# THE INNOCENT PARTY

Other Books by John Hawkes

*The Blood Oranges*
*The Cannibal*
*The Beetle Leg*
*Death, Sleep & the Traveler*
*The Goose on the Grave & The Owl*
*The Lime Twig*
*Lunar Landscapes*
*The Owl*
*Second Skin*
*Travesty*

# THE INNOCENT PARTY

Four Short Plays by John Hawkes

Preface by Herbert Blau

A New Directions Book

Copyright © 1966 by John Hawkes
Library of Congress catalog card number: 66-27614
ISBN: 0-8112-0064-7
Published simultaneously in Canada by
McClelland and Stewart Ltd.
All rights reserved.

The author is grateful to the Ford Foundation and to Herbert Blau and Jules Irving, co-founders of The Actor's Workshop of San Francisco, for the gift of a year in the theater.

CAUTION: *Professionals and amateurs are hereby warned that these plays, being fully protected under the copyright laws of the United States of America, the British Empire including the Dominion of Canada, and all other countries of the Copyright Union, are subject to royalty. All rights, including professional, amateur, motion picture, recitation, lecturing, public reading, radio-broadcasting, and the rights of translation into foreign languages, are strictly reserved. Particular emphasis is laid on the question of readings, permission for which must be secured from the author's agent in writing. All inquiries should be addressed to the author's agent, Harold Ober Associates, Inc., 40 East 49, New York City.*

Manufactured in the United States of America

New Directions Books are published for James Laughlin
by New Directions Publishing Corporation,
333 Sixth Avenue, New York 10014

THIRD PRINTING

For
Jack
Sophie
Calvert
and Richard

## CONTENTS

| | |
|---|---|
| Preface BY HERBERT BLAU | 9 |
| *The Innocent Party* | 13 |
| *The Wax Museum* | 97 |
| *The Undertaker* | 135 |
| *The Questions* | 169 |

# PREFACE by Herbert Blau

The year before we came to New York, John Hawkes arrived in San Francisco to be with our theater. Jules Irving and I read the novels before he came. They were luminous with atrocity. I thought I read somewhere he lived in a baronial old house in Rhode Island; no doubt there were bats in the masonry. One invents a nightmare and gets a rude awakening. Crew-cut, garrulous, he was about as gothic as a fraternity pledge. Where did all that terror come from? We were like the publicans in Synge's play who marvel at the strange gap between a gallows story and the wide-eyed teller of it.

Jack came to rehearsals, the innocent party, attending on the event. He never pretended to be anything but a novice. The humility is important. Various novelists are now trying their hand at the drama; it is very promising. Except that some of them, with the condescension of Old Masters, are using their left hand. It won't work. The drama is a ruthless form. As Henry James discovered, it demands of the novelist that he be willing to throw his best cargo overboard to save the ship. It also demands peaceful coexistence with the inscrutable art of acting.

Jack was willing, Jack was there. He sat with incredible patience through rehearsals even of the plays he disliked. What we could have done without, he wouldn't have missed for the world. The very tedium of the worst rehearsals struck him as the thing itself. He responded to the collective feel of the form. He came as an observer and became a participant, the director's alter ego. Crouched over his notes, scenting, he bristled enthusiasm, bridled at error. Jack was the ubiquitous dog that's friend to men, with his nails he dug it up again. In midnight postmortems at the sort of tacky drive-in where the owner's eyes are "like beef soup," he read us the riot act. "Why that's almost a sacrament, man, they can't just *say* it!" Like the hunting dogs in *The Questions*, he was often ahead of the pace but rarely aside from the quarry. There was never arrogance. The innocence took a reflective gape and let fly, wondering.

In Hawkes' plays, as in his novels, there is an inscape of wonder in a landscape of mutilations. Innocence is on the limb, ripe for perversion. Brute ignorance encroaches. We see deadness descending upon the gift of play. Whether he knows it or not, the new form in which Hawkes is working does double duty for his theme. There is a time-serving brutality in the theater, which confounds playing with acting. In the theater you must play, but *play before your time is up*. There is an alluring dark humor in the warning: "It's the witching hour in the wax museum, Sally Ann. It's time for love."

The territory of Hawkes' concern is "emotional oblivion." "I've spent my life," says the undertaker, "disposing of the remains." Hawkes writes of dead passions, exuberantly, with a mortician's care. He can glamorize a carcass. There is a penumbra of immortal longing around brute fact. Hawkes' novel *The Lime Twig* opens with the gossip columnist Sidney Slyter, dispenser of dead emotions, writing of "light returning to the faces of heroic stone." One remembers the heisted horse, stiff in a sling, like a giant weathervane in cold moonlight. If he can make a wild animal palpably marmoreal, he can put a patina of bright gold over slick metal. In the androgynous world of *The Innocent Party* there is an unforgettable aura about the white Cadillac of the lesbian aunt "in the mist under the acacia tree." The process can also be reversed. Metamorphosis may come over us like saran wrap. The sweat of a woman is "like a kind of beauty cream."

It takes dispassion to write it either way: "whoever heard of being pure without being coldblooded too?" The pathos of the plays is in the distance between coldbloodedness and nostalgia. "Go think about the Negroes and the seeds of death," says the undertaker to his son. *The Questions* does that, but the father in that play "had this virginity business on the mind. . . ." So does Jack Hawkes. History, said Freud, is the slow return of the repressed; in Hawkes the return is in, bursting with bitter fruit. Or to change the image: we see the antebellum lady at the hunt, "wrists cocked like little tawny angels," going in for the sensual kill.

The virginity business is part of the haunted waste of the American dream. "I hope you find your soul on the *Santa Maria*," says a character in *The Innocent Party*. Hawkes writes about these longings with the astonished luxuriance of the first voyagers. In the sudden but casual crossbreeding of erotic fantasy and myth, the deadness is redeemed: "soul is practically meaningless," but in certain contexts "it still comes at you like a little corkscrew of lightning from Thor himself. . . ."

At the exhausted motel of *The Innocent Party*, there's not a ripple in the pool. The father and mother are "nothing but a couple of dead Christians from the time of peepot morality." The daughter, however, a product of the virginity business, is something more than that. Jane, the nymphet, is a cellular growth. With her, we are at the bare moral midriff of the kandy-kolored tangerine-flaked streamlined ethos, which others celebrate and Hawkes sees coming up the drainpipe like a centipede. There is a chamber of horrors below the wax museum. The other side of innocence is demonism. Hawkes' dialogue reads sometimes like a phantom's gasp—arias of audacious desperation, emotionally spent, gasping out a last testament.

Two of the plays—*The Innocent Party* and *The Wax Museum*—were written before we all left San Francisco. We did *The Wax Museum* in a studio performance. The other two he sent me last June from Sanibel Island, down in the Gulf in Florida. He described *The Undertaker* as a "farcical melodrama" based on the father's suicide in *Second Skin*. "The longer one—*The Questions*—seems to be some kind of terrible madness." If so, it's a madness to act upon. Most new plays, hard on the ear, heavy on the heart, merely plod on stage. Terror be praised, it's a pleasure to read some plays that sing. It makes them worth imagining in the theater.

*New York City*
*April 1966*

# THE INNOCENT PARTY

*Patio of an abandoned motel in a subtropical area of the United States. Upstage right is a dried-out swimming pool partially filled with debris. A hammock is slung downstage left.*

JANE. *The daughter. She is an adolescent, part tomboy and part Aphrodite-as-young-girl, and as such approaches a mythic force. Throughout the action she wears a bikini, usually carries a transistor radio.*

PHOEBE. *The aunt. Sportswoman, sophisticate, world traveler, heiress, she is bold and beautiful and in general manages to capitalize on her masculinity.*

BEATRIX. *The mother. She is a strong but empty person in the midst of ruin. She holds herself under a tight psychic rein, is dressed throughout in a shabby blood-red negligee.*

EDWARD. *The father. A few years older than his sister Phoebe, he radiates the pure spirit and gentleness and benevolence of someone whose failure in life has been unspectacular but complete. He collects sea shells, wears a worn white linen suit.*

## SCENE 1

*Dawn. Lights up on Jane, who is standing at the edge of the pool, and on Phoebe, who lies smoking her first cigarette of the day in the hammock where she has spent the night. Phoebe wears only a black brassiere and Bermuda shorts and is partially covered by a lightweight Mexican blanket. Her bright orange man's silk sport shirt is on the back of one of the patio chairs, her enormous hand-tooled leather purse is standing on the patio table. The oppressive heat of the new day is already apparent. Jane squats slowly and stares into the pool. She is wearing her bikini.*

JANE:
>  Not a ripple.

PHOEBE:
>  You say something, Jane?

JANE:
>  Not a ripple.
>  (*Pause*)
>  Do you know what's wrong with this pool, Aunt Phoebe?

PHOEBE:
>  Wrong with it? The swimming pool is—out of order?
>  (*She laughs*)
>  You make it sound like an old plugged-up john in the little girls' room.

(*Pause*)
Well, what's the matter with it?

JANE:
No water. That's the matter. It's dry.

PHOEBE:
Bone dry?

JANE:
If I shut my eyes and jumped into it I'd break a leg.

PHOEBE:
Don't jump. Please, it's too early.
(*Pause*)
What do you think, Jane, has it got a leak or something?

JANE:
It's not a toilet in a lavatory. It's a swimming pool. I'm serious, Aunt Phoebe.

PHOEBE:
Of course you are. But I'm here now, Jane. Shall we call in a plumber?

JANE:
It needs more than a plumber.

PHOEBE:
Yes. Well, I'll take you swimming somewhere else.

JANE:
I want to swim here. I could be a mermaid in my own pool. I could be Tarzan's companion in the water. I could go under holding my breath and skim around the bottom like a baby shark. I'd come up spouting!

PHOEBE:

Look out for the alligators.

JANE:

But it's dry. See there? A dirty old palmetto leaf, a rake, a rubber boot—what kind of a pool is that? And I'll tell you something, Aunt Phoebe. Mother dumps ashes in it.

PHOEBE:

We better condemn it then. From now on no one goes near the pool. Anyway, who wants a pool without boys?

JANE:

She could dump her butts and ashes somewhere else.

PHOEBE:

I suppose she could. But what about a nice boy to sit on the end of the diving board, Janie? Wouldn't you like that?

JANE:

If I saw a boy on that diving board I'd knock him off!

PHOEBE:

Good God. . . . I hope you're not thinking of attacking your poor aunt, Janie. I've always been fond of you, baby. Remember that.

JANE:

Listen, Aunt Phoebe, I'm trying to tell you something. I come out here every morning, before it's light. I stand here and I touch myself—on the arms, the legs—touch myself like that a few times even though it's still hot from the day before and I can hardly move. Then I hold my hand in front of my face until I see it. Then I sniff because I want to know if I can smell the flowers. Then I listen, and I think I'll hear it trickling, or I think I'll hear drops of it dripping at the edge. And you know what? I think of fish and whales and seaweed and big jellyfish sitting like eggs without shells in little pools of water. I listen and don't hear anything but the doves. Still I think it's filling up—maybe it's already reached the top—and I start walking over to it. Usually I smack into something in the dark. And then, listening and holding my breath, Aunt Phoebe, I kneel down at the edge and think I'm going to pop out of my bikini. And do you know what I'm looking at?

PHOEBE:
No, baby.

JANE:
Me! For a moment there's water in the pool and leaning over like that I see myself, Aunt Phoebe, my own face. But by then it's light, so I go and sit on the end of the diving board and make it squeak up and down in the sunlight. The mat on the end of the board is spongy.

PHOEBE:
Spongy? Spongy? My God. . . . Were you out here doing all that this morning, Jane?

JANE:
> This morning was like all the rest. I saw my own face, Aunt Phoebe.

PHOEBE:
> While I was asleep in the hammock?

JANE:
> Yes, yes. I even forgot you were there.

PHOEBE:
> Janie. . . . Tomorrow morning your Aunt Phoebe will wake up. I'll watch you, Janie.

JANE:
> You can hear the doves right now, if you listen.

PHOEBE:
> The hell with the doves, baby. I've been all over the world. I just want to see your pool filling up with water. I want to see your reflection in it. That'll be enough for me, baby.

JANE:
> There's never any water in this pool. It's dry. It went dry before I was born.

PHOEBE:
> Never mind. I'll take care of it.

JANE:
> You'd have to know about pipes and valves and water mains. It's hopeless.

PHOEBE:
> Your old aunt's been around the world, baby. Don't worry.

JANE:

But we need some kind of engineer. It's hopeless.

PHOEBE:

Never mind. My own pool was made of marble. What do you think of that? It was big enough for water skiing. Ever done any snorkeling, Janie? I used to snorkel in my pool. It had a high board as well as a regular board, it had a gadget for controlling the temperature. So I know something about swimming pools. And I know something about boys, too.

JANE:

A high board, Aunt Phoebe? Really high? Was it a twenty-footer?

PHOEBE:

Sure, baby. You could jump a horse off it. And you should have seen the boys who used to hang around my pool. European-style trunks, Janie. European trunks.

JANE:

I'm not interested in European trunks. I've got a bikini myself.

PHOEBE:

I see you, baby.

JANE:

I got this bikini from a magazine.

PHOEBE:

Smart girl. You would have liked that pool of mine. I even had a private lifeguard.

**JANE:**

I wouldn't want a lifeguard to rescue me, Aunt Phoebe. I'd rather drown.

**PHOEBE:**

He was an ex-Marine with a sun helmet and a whistle on a cord. He was a beautiful lifeguard, Janie. We put a chemical in the water and if anyone forgot himself—you know how young boys sometimes forget themselves in the water—why the chemical reaction was like an explosion. The water changed color—it turned bright orange, Janie—my lifeguard saw it and blew his whistle, we made everyone get out of the pool until the water-changer did its job. No one ever peed twice in your auntie's pool, Jane. I can tell you that. It was a marble pool and it was sanitary.

**JANE:**

I guess I would have peed in it like the boys. Mother thinks I'm queer and awkward and unpredictable. I would have peed in your pool.

**PHOEBE:**

Don't you believe it, baby. You're a dream. But do you know what those young boys did? They played water polo. They kicked and splashed and jackknifed in and out of that deep clear water as if they were my own sons. Sometimes they even tore each other's trunks off. Aunt Phoebe's amateur water polo tournament, that's what it was. I used to watch them with the lifeguard, up on his stand. I used to blow kisses to them. It was hilarious.

JANE:
> You wouldn't have blown any kisses to me.

PHOEBE:
> Oh yes I would, baby. I would have blown kisses to you and one of the boys would have hugged you when you were dripping wet.

JANE:
> Aunt Phoebe, listen. . . .

PHOEBE:
> Yes, Jane?

JANE:
> There's nobody here but me.

PHOEBE:
> And now me. Now me.

JANE:
> I can do the deadman's float.

PHOEBE:
> Really, Jane? You can show me. Tomorrow morning, early, before it's light.

JANE:
> You'll see. I'll be a shark on the bottom and a deadman on the surface. Upside down.

PHOEBE:
> We'll meet out here together. First we'll look at our faces in the water, then we'll swim. And we'll be quiet, Janie, we won't make a sound.

JANE:
> Phoebe?

PHOEBE:
> Jane?

JANE:
> May I call you Phoebe?

PHOEBE:
> Mermaids use first names, Janie. But only when they're alone. Only when they're in the water together. Alone.

BEATRIX:
> (*offstage*)
> Are you awake, Phoebe?

EDWARD:
> (*offstage*)
> Coffee, Phoebe.

BEATRIX:
> (*offstage*)
> Are you decent?

PHOEBE:
> (*pitching her cigarette across the stage into the pool*)
> My shirt and pocketbook, Janie. Hand them over. And don't drop the pocketbook, baby. It's full of loot.

# SCENE 2

*Jane has worked her way from the pool to the hammock. Now she gives Phoebe the shirt and pocketbook and walks slowly and in a suddenly provocative fashion to an old canvas deck chair beside the pool where she stretches out in her habitual pose and picks up her radio which, softly, she begins to play. Enter Beatrix, carrying a bunch of hibiscus, scissors and a mason jar, and Edward, carrying a coffee tray. It is obvious that Edward has dressed himself in his crumpled white linen suit in the dark. He looks away when he sees that his sister is not fully clothed.*

EDWARD:
> The sun's bright already. But we didn't mean to wake you, Phoebe. We tried to be quiet.

BEATRIX:
> We rise early.

EDWARD:
> Old people can't sleep, can they, Phoebe. But at least we didn't rattle the pans.

PHOEBE:
> I didn't hear a thing. My God, were you whispering? It wasn't necessary, Edward. Not on my account.

*(Phoebe drops the pocketbook into the hammock and puts on her shirt which, however, she leaves unbuttoned*

*and hanging loose outside her shorts. Then she rummages in a large white calfskin suitcase for a pair of sandals, silk neckerchief, etc.*)

**EDWARD:**
> Oh we didn't talk, Phoebe. We didn't say anything.

**BEATRIX:**
> We wanted to talk about you, love. But we restrained ourselves.

**PHOEBE:**
> That wasn't necessary.

**BEATRIX:**
> (*cutting the flowers one by one, arranging them in the mason jar*)
> Were you quiet, Jane? You didn't wake your Aunt Phoebe, did you?

**EDWARD:**
> Jane treasures her radio. Some girls read or listen to sea shells, Jane listens to jazz. We try not to mind.

**PHOEBE:**
> (*to Jane*)
> What can you pick up, baby? Ever hear them broadcasting from Baby Green's Evening in Paris? Can you get New Orleans?

**BEATRIX:**
> I asked her to be quiet this morning, Phoebe.

**EDWARD:**
> Coffee, Phoebe? Sugar and cream?

PHOEBE:
> Black for the black sheep, baby.

BEATRIX:
> (*holding up a blossom*)
> Aren't they lovely? At least we have flowers. Edward and I went out and cut them together—for you, Phoebe—before it was even light.

PHOEBE:
> For me, Beatrix. My God. You haven't changed.

EDWARD:
> Out there, out in the mist and shadows, do you know what we saw?

PHOEBE:
> Jane's secret boyfriend, is that it? Have you got a boyfriend, Janie?

JANE:
> (*dreaming*)
> No, Phoebe, no. . . .

EDWARD:
> Your car!

BEATRIX:
> Your white Cadillac. Is it new, Phoebe?

PHOEBE:
> Brand-new. It's got my initials on the door. Happy birthday from Phoebe to Phoebe.

EDWARD:
> It was standing there in the mist under the acacia tree.

BEATRIX:
> What do you think he did? He took out his handkerchief and tried to wipe a little clear spot on one of the windows. Can you imagine Edward trying to wipe away the mist with his handkerchief?
> (*She laughs.*)

EDWARD:
> *Your* car, Phoebe. It was so big and white. I couldn't believe it, couldn't believe my eyes. You were really here. I wanted to see inside.

BEATRIX:
> We don't have an automobile. Edward and I are so old-fashioned.

(*Jane rolls her head from side to side in her dream and laughs.*)

PHOEBE:
> The keys are yours, dear brother, as long as I'm here.

BEATRIX:
> We want you to stay with us, Phoebe. Don't leave....

PHOEBE:
> A couple of days, three days. I won't impose.

BEATRIX:
> (*smiling, collecting herself*)
> But Edward couldn't drive a white Cadillac. And I wouldn't think of trying. Do you remember when you gave me a few lessons on the dirt road behind your father's house? I was so inept.

EDWARD:
> Your golf clubs were on the back seat, there was a folded newspaper, your tennis racket. Even one of your gorgeous undergarments, which I'm afraid I did notice, Phoebe. I saw it all and I couldn't speak. I was too happy.

JANE:
> (*dreaming, rolling her head*)
> Fink, fink, fink. . . .

BEATRIX:
> Do you always leave your car locked, love? How thoughtful. The world *is* full of vandals, isn't it.

PHOEBE:
> I was robbed in Carson City, as a matter of fact. Cleaned out.

BEATRIX:
> Poor Phoebe.

PHOEBE:
> I saw the whole thing. He was a bewhiskered old devil with a donkey. Packed all my stuff on the donkey and rushed off into the hills. The old devil. A girl can't be too careful. You never know who's going to rob you blind.

EDWARD:
> I wanted to see inside more than anything in the world, Phoebe. I had to look. I couldn't say a word.

BEATRIX:
> Edward was so moved he couldn't even help me with the flowers. I had to cut them myself.

**EDWARD:**

> We stopped again on the way back. And it was still there, Phoebe, still there. My own sister's car with unmistakable tire tracks approaching up the road to the acacia tree.

**BEATRIX:**

> Edward is so meticulous, Phoebe. So patient. He reacts with, with spiritual shivers. I could hardly tear him away.

**EDWARD:**

> I'm still blinded with your arrival. I don't trust myself. The lights, the noise, your hand waving out of the car window, the sound of the horn. . . . And then all night I heard you sleeping out here in the hammock, and suddenly—at dawn—I knew a little sleep might have destroyed it all. I might have been dreaming. So I looked into the car when I saw it, and when we came back with the flowers I was afraid it would be gone. But here you are. I'm still trembling.

**BEATRIX:**

> She's going to stay with us, Edward. Don't worry.

**PHOEBE:**

> All right, you two. Let's celebrate! We'll have a real party, a reunion, a vacation together. Old Phoebe's the angel of joy, you two. Remember that!

**EDWARD:**

> A celebration!

BEATRIX:

   (*brightly*)
   Yes, you are an angel. You haven't changed.

JANE:

   (*dreaming*)
   A party! A ball! And plenty of that Acapulco gold! Oh my God, my God . . . what a crazy dream . . . !

(*She laughs, the raucous rock-and-roll swells on the radio. Edward worries, fidgets, rises in uncertainty and embarrassment and moves to Jane on tiptoe, leans down and whispers. The music subsides, Edward returns to the table.*)

EDWARD:

   I used to listen to sea shells when I was a young person. I still do.

BEATRIX:

   Sometimes Jane seems to want to drown us out, Phoebe. But when she listens to *Comic Strip of the Air* it's worse. Much worse. I can't stand to hear humorous sexual stories for young people. I really can't.

EDWARD:

   But we try not to mind.

PHOEBE:

   (*as the music rises and falls*)
   Quiet, baby! Tone it down!

(*Jane laughs. Edward stands, impulsively removes the flowers from the mason jar and, one by one and with great care, rearranges them in the jar.*)

**EDWARD:**
> So here you are, Phoebe. You've come to us. From another world.

**BEATRIX:**
> And here we are, Phoebe. In all our—poverty!

**EDWARD:**
> You mean our pride, Beatrix, our gentle pride.

**BEATRIX:**
> Phoebe knows what I mean.

**EDWARD:**
> Seven years, Phoebe. With only your postcards to tell us you were alive. So many years of separation—were they necessary?

**PHOEBE:**
> I went around the world, baby. I took my time.

**BEATRIX:**
> You went around the world while Edward sold box cameras and Jane—our incomprehensible Jane—multiplied before our eyes, cell by cell. While we watched she grew. Yes, grew.
> (*She shudders.*)
> I don't know how, or why.

**PHOEBE:**
> And you, Beatrix?

**BEATRIX:**
> Never mind about me. Welcome home.

**EDWARD:**

I wasn't ashamed to sell cameras door to door. Should I have been? What's wrong with selling good dollar cameras that took honest, clear pictures on inexpensive film? I sold cameras, Phoebe, until—until I went under. I must tell you, Phoebe—just one more word on this subject. I still don't know how it happened. But when I *went under* I knew I had reached the end. And I was glad. Glad. I was finished and I became myself.

**BEATRIX:**

Welcome home, Phoebe.

**EDWARD:**

Were you ashamed to go around the world, Phoebe? You needn't have been. It's just that you were away too long. Much too long.

**BEATRIX:**

During your travels, Phoebe, did you become yourself? When Edward *went under* at least he took Jane and me with him. And Jane was growing—before our eyes—and I . . . I was barren but beautiful.

(*Jane laughs.*)

**EDWARD:**

Beatrix, please. . . .
(*He holds up a flower.*)
This one is just a bit too long, isn't it? A shade too long.
(*Elaborately, he snips the stem with the scissors.*)

BEATRIX:
> No, let me say it, for Phoebe's benefit. There is a special beauty in barrenness. Edward never understood my condition. Edward sank, but Jane and I suffered in other ways.

JANE:
> (*dreaming*)
> I want to *go under* too!

EDWARD:
> The doctor kept nothing from me, Beatrix. He said you were a lovely woman and that I should be proud of you. He was right.
> (*He holds up the flower.*)
> I hope you weren't ashamed, Phoebe. I was proud of you too.

BEATRIX:
> (*to Phoebe*)
> Did you find yourself? Did you? Did you eat well? And drink wine? And dance on deck in the moonlight? Did you see your own face in the stupid, oh stupid face of a camel? Did you have fun, Phoebe?
> (*Jane moans and writhes.*)
> Alone out there, traveling those cruise lanes around the world with strangers while your own brother went down with his wife and child from motel to cheap motel—did you really hold your head up like the camel, Phoebe? Was it really fun?

PHOEBE:
> You bet your life it was fun. And don't forget this, you two: I had the fare.

BEATRIX:

In your hand-tooled pocketbook.

PHOEBE:

In my pocketbook. And in five banks.

BEATRIX:

Edward has never been inside a bank except to arrange for a loan.
(*She laughs.*)
And when he *went under* there were no more loans.

PHOEBE:

Why didn't he come crawling to sister? Old Phoebe's the angel of joy—remember?

BEATRIX:

You were always so generous, Phoebe.

EDWARD:

And so beautiful, beautiful—like an Indian princess or an Egyptian queen!

BEATRIX:

(*to Edward*)
Yes, she's beautiful. And why not? Wasn't she sailing around out there on the *Santa Maria*—that's what the first card said, the *Santa Maria!*—while I was sitting here with a smile on my face and turning black inside?

EDWARD:

You're not black inside. You never were.

BEATRIX:
> Barren.
> (*She laughs.*)
> A barren woman.
> (*to Phoebe*)
> Well, I hope it was worthwhile. I hope you found your soul on the *Santa Maria*, I hope you enjoyed yourself. In seven years you didn't even remember Jane at Christmas time....

JANE:
> (*dreaming*)
> I'm OK, Phoebe, I'm OK....

EDWARD:
> My sister has never had any need to be ashamed, she has always been beautiful....

BEATRIX:
> And free. And generous. And strong. With her black hair and flashing eyes and white teeth and smile like the leer of some animal and her bosom, her embarrassing bosom...!

PHOEBE:
> Now wait a minute. Now wait a minute....

BEATRIX:
> Oh I could cry for you, Phoebe....

EDWARD:
> Please, please.... I used to lie awake in the dark, Phoebe, thinking of you and wondering how you

were and smiling at the thought of you promenading, living, and a curious single question always came to my mind: did the ship roll, Phoebe? Did it roll softly and gently across a dark sea?

(*Jane laughs. The radio booms and fades. Edward glances at his daughter and smiles at her helplessly.*)

PHOEBE:
>(*pausing*)
>Yes. Yes, it rolled.

EDWARD:
>I thought it did.

BEATRIX:
>While you stood at the rail and sipped wine.

EDWARD:
>Tell us, Phoebe. Please tell us.

PHOEBE:
>My adventures . . . ?

BEATRIX:
>Your adventures, love. . . .

(*The music increases in volume, shifts subtly from rock-and-roll to jazz-like parody of orchestrated sexual themes and love songs of the world. Slowly Jane swings to a sitting position, stares at Phoebe. Edward looks at his daughter, smiles, puts his finger to his lips in a gesture asking for silence. Phoebe lights a cigarette, glances at the hot sky, wipes her forehead, seems about to remove the orange shirt, turns downstage left. The radio grows nearly silent.*)

PHOEBE:
> Seven years ago I went down to pier number whatever it was . . . .

BEATRIX:
> . . . . in your two-piece tweed traveling outfit.

PHOEBE:
> In my silver lamé evening gown, baby. Please.

BEATRIX:
> You had first-class passage . . . .

PHOEBE:
> . . . . around the world. A suite on the upper deck all to myself.

BEATRIX:
> It was filled with flowers . . . .

PHOEBE:
> *Bon Voyage* from my lawyer.

BEATRIX:
> A steward brought champagne . . . .

PHOEBE:
> . . . . in a silver bucket.

BEATRIX:
> You heard sirens and whistles in the darkness.

PHOEBE:
> It was a midnight sailing.

BEATRIX:
> The orchestra was playing . . . .

PHOEBE:

    . . . . and my little taxi driver stood on the pier.

BEATRIX:

    He waved goodby!

*(Jane's face grows bright with pleasure. She rises slowly, stands as if at the ship's rail and begins to wave, timidly at first and then feverishly.)*

PHOEBE:

    He waved goodby.

BEATRIX:

    You turned away . . . .

PHOEBE:

    . . . . and a passing sailor whistled at me, baby.

BEATRIX:

    In the ballroom they were dancing. . . .

PHOEBE:

    . . . . and I joined them.

BEATRIX:

    You waltzed the rest of the night . . . .

*(Jane begins awkwardly to waltz.)*

PHOEBE:

    . . . . with a young man who turned out to be the ship's lifeguard!

*(She laughs, and Jane imitates the laugh.)*

BEATRIX:

    You ate together . . . .

PHOEBE:
> Chicken, duck, squab, little birds shot off the coast of Scotland.

BEATRIX:
> And when the sun came up, he kissed you!

(*Jane pantomimes the kiss.*)

PHOEBE:
> Nobody ever kissed me like that lifeguard, baby. He had a sun helmet and a whistle on a cord.

BEATRIX:
> And in the days that followed you played volleyball together, made spectacles of yourselves in the ship's pool, stood indecently close together on the prow in the wind.

(*Jane pantomimes these actions.*)

PHOEBE:
> (*stepping on her cigarette and again turning upstage*)
> I sailed away.

BEATRIX:
> (*rising and facing her*)
> Yes, you sailed away.

(*Jane collapses slowly and again stretches out in the deck chair.*)

EDWARD:
> It must have been wonderful, Phoebe.

BEATRIX:
>    (*Pause*)
>    It was disgusting.

(*The rock-and-roll becomes more audible.*)

EDWARD:
>    And now you've come to us!
>    (*Pause*)

BEATRIX:
>    (*dramatically*)
>    Of course the question, Phoebe, is whether you've come to help us.

EDWARD:
>    Please, please ....
>    (*to Phoebe*)
>    I want to show you my collection of Murex shells. Did you know that the Murex is a large family of marine carnivorous mollusks of high organization? They creep and swim, chiefly in warm seas. Did you know that in the Murex the sexes are distinct, Phoebe? Isn't that wonderful?
>    (*Pause*)

BEATRIX:
>    Have you come to help us, Phoebe?

PHOEBE:
>    I don't know what you're talking about.

BEATRIX:
>    Help, help, help! Don't you recognize a desperate cry when you hear one, Phoebe?

PHOEBE:
> What do you want? What do you expect from me?

BEATRIX:
> Generosity, my love. Generosity, self-sacrifice, assistance. We're the last of the charity cases—aren't we, Edward.

EDWARD:
> The genus Murex overshadows all the others in size, elaborateness of decoration, and number of species .... I'll show you a few examples, Phoebe. They're amazing.

BEATRIX:
> (*to Phoebe*)
> We're destitute! Isn't it amusing, Phoebe? We live on bones out of a tin pot!

EDWARD:
> Please, please, Beatrix, think of Jane ....

(*Jane laughs.*)

BEATRIX:
> Yes, Jane! Jane knows what it is to be poor! Like her mother.

PHOEBE:
> Oh for God's sake!

BEATRIX:
> Do you doubt me, Phoebe? Look at her, open your eyes. Jane has no clothes, can't you see that? And Edward has one suit to his name. And your sister-in-

law is forced to look like a woman of, of ill-fame. Does it please you, Phoebe? Does it?

PHOEBE:
(*laughing*)
You've never looked better. All three of you.

EDWARD:
(*embarrassed*)
There's a certain truth in what she says about Jane.
(*Pause*)
Jane used to have a little velvet bow that we clipped in her hair....

BEATRIX:
But not any more, Phoebe. Not any more.

EDWARD:
And she used to have pink babydoll pajamas....

BEATRIX:
No more. No more babydoll pajamas!

EDWARD:
And a little satin rollerskating skirt and matching underpants....

PHOEBE:
What perversity.

EDWARD:
She grew up, you see, and now there's nothing. The yellow frock for Sunday school, the organdy bonnet, the little black patent-leather shoes—it's all gone, Phoebe, isn't that strange?

PHOEBE:
> With a body like that, who cares?

(*Jane sits bolt upright and smiles broadly.*)

BEATRIX:
> What you don't know, Phoebe, is that my daughter has been stealing from the Negroes.

PHOEBE:
> (*laughing*)
> Good for Jane.

EDWARD:
> But stealing, Phoebe....

PHOEBE:
> She's smart and quick and strong and pretty—you ought to be proud!

(*The radio roars and dies, Jane leaps to her feet and struts up and down; she claps her hands in pantomime.*)

BEATRIX:
> Of course she's driven to stealing. I realize Edward and I are responsible for what she does. Children of the poor in spirit turn to stealing.

PHOEBE:
> I'll take her away with me. How's that?

BEATRIX:
> Charity at last? How kind.

(*Jane cavorts gleefully.*)

PHOEBE:
> Jane's my favorite.

**BEATRIX:**
> Dear, sweet, generous Phoebe.

**PHOEBE:**
> Even when she was a little child I loved her.

(*Jane freezes.*)

**BEATRIX:**
> But did you love your brother, Phoebe? Did you love me?

**PHOEBE:**
> There was always something special about Janie, even then. She burns in my mind still, that little flaming babe! If poor Caliban had ever gotten hold of lovely Ariel, you two . . . .
> (*She laughs.*)
> Jane would have been their natural child. She was both animal and angel even then. My God!

(*Jane happily pantomimes mock evil and beatific attitudes.*)

**BEATRIX:**
> And now she steals!

**PHOEBE:**
> She's a virgin. She doesn't know whether she wants to be a girl or boy. But she'll find out. I used to love Janie when her hair was chopped off above her little ears and when her little bellybutton stuck out above the elastic of her panties. I loved her then and I love her now. And now she's grown. A sweet, strong, nubile creature—my God, my God!

(*Jane stands rigidly and happily at attention.*)

EDWARD:
>But she steals from the Negro children down the road. You wouldn't believe it. And the worst of it is that whatever she brings home—a rag doll, a tin automobile, a freshly laundered undershirt, a fishing pole—whatever she brings home, Phoebe, she destroys. Is there nothing we can do, Phoebe? Nothing at all?

(*Jane remains at attention but appears dismayed.*)

BEATRIX:
>Nothing. There's no hope for Jane. My barren womanhood cries out when I say it, Phoebe—but I have always feared for Jane. And now I'm convinced of it—there's no hope for Jane. A girl who spends her waking hours almost nude will someday do something terrible.
>(*slowly*)
>Someday our Jane is going to do something terrible. She's dangerous.

PHOEBE:
>You're out of your mind, baby! But I've told you already, Jane's going away with me.

(*Jane hugs herself, again collapses slowly into the deck chair.*)

BEATRIX:
>Yes. Perhaps she'll even sail off with you on the *Santa Maria*. Yes, of course. But what about your own brother? What about his wife?

PHOEBE:

>(*slowly*)
>You don't look destitute to me.
>(*brightly*)
>Now if you had been robbed by an old son-of-a-bitch with a donkey, I might understand.

(*Jane laughs.*)

EDWARD:

>Phoebe, please .... the child.

BEATRIX:

>You don't believe me! A retired insipid brother and his cankerous wife deserve only your mockery, is that it? All right. All right. Show her your elbows, Edward, show her the seat of your pants.

PHOEBE:

>No exhibitions, please.

BEATRIX:

>Go on, Edward. Swallow your pride, that little dead goldfish of yours called pride.

(*Edward smiles nervously, then lifts each elbow, studies it, turns and bends over and slowly hoists the bottom of his jacket. The volume of the radio increases. After a pause he straightens up, rearranges his clothing with little tugs, runs a hand through his hair, smiles. Beatrix assists this self-inspection.*)

BEATRIX:

>Satisfied, Phoebe? Your brother—your own brother—threadbare in the elbows and out in the seat of his pants.

PHOEBE:
>(*laughing*)
>It suits his character. Did you ever see a really sweet man who wasn't careless about his clothes? Edward's radiance shines through the rip in his pants, baby. He hasn't changed.

BEATRIX:
>(*moving close to Phoebe*)
>Touch me, Phoebe. Smell my breath.
>(*Phoebe does not move.*)
>Do you like the color of my gown? Do you like the torn ruffles? Do you like my hair? I cut it with the kitchen scissors, Phoebe. I curl it with an iron I heat on the stove. But let me show you my scars....
>(*She gestures as if to untie the negligee.*)
>my scars of ignominy. Oh, I have a pair of stockings—I'll show them to you—but right now my legs are bare. Bare and starved! Look at them. Take a good look at my wobbling knees. They're like shrunken heads, aren't they, Phoebe? Breathe deeply, you beautiful traveler. Smell it? Smell it? That's not "My Sin" you smell on my body, Phoebe. It's something else.

EDWARD:
>The doctor said you were a lovely woman.

BEATRIX:
>I haven't been to a doctor in years. Believe me, Phoebe, I need to go to a doctor. But we can't even eat.

EDWARD:
> Tell her she's a lovely woman—she won't listen to me.

BEATRIX:
> Touch me, Phoebe! Turn me to gold!

(*Phoebe submits reluctantly to her sister-in-law's passionate embrace, then roughly disengages herself.*)

PHOEBE:
> (*brightly*)
> Listen, you two. I didn't come empty-handed!

EDWARD:
> My sister—my Indian princess, my Egyptian queen!

PHOEBE:
> Did you think I'd come empty-handed? Not old Phoebe.

BEATRIX:
> Dear, sweet, benevolent Phoebe.

PHOEBE:
> We're going to have a party, remember? Look here. (*She rummages in suitcase, sets three liquor bottles on the table.*)
> Tequila! The best there is!
> (*Pause*)

EDWARD:
> Beatrix and I don't drink.

PHOEBE:
> Well, baby, it's time you began.

**BEATRIX:**
> Yes. It's time we began.

**PHOEBE:**
> We have to get off on the right foot, don't we? So tonight we kill the tequila.

**BEATRIX:**
> Oh marvelous!

**EDWARD:**
> I don't know, Phoebe. Do you think we should?

**PHOEBE:**
> Come on, come on, we'll enjoy ourselves.

**BEATRIX:**
> Of course we will.

**PHOEBE:**
> Listen, you two. We've got to have some supplies. Let's send Janie out in the Cadillac for supplies, OK? Razor blades, facial cream, tissues, candles, a country ham—the works. Tonight we kill the tequila at a banquet, OK?

**BEATRIX:**
> Welcome home, Phoebe!

**EDWARD:**
> (*smiling*)
> But now we'll sleep. Down here we always observe the siesta, Phoebe.

**PHOEBE:**
> We'll take our siestas and Janie can go for the supplies.

(*She digs laboriously into her pocketbook, hands Edward the car keys and a few bills.*)

**BEATRIX:**
You've come to help us. Thank God.

**PHOEBE:**
(*grinning*)
We'll see. We'll see about that.

**EDWARD:**
Siesta, Phoebe. Siesta!

(*Exit Beatrix with flowers, Edward with the coffee tray. Phoebe, still grinning, stares at Jane, who after several moments of apparent sleep bolts after her parents.*)

**JANE:**
Hey, Dad! Dad! Wait for me!

# SCENE 3

*Phoebe muses, takes a long drink from one of the bottles, then slowly removes her shirt and sandals. She stretches and lies down again in the hammock. With hands behind her head she swings lazily, while from Jane's radio, offstage, comes sounds of a guitar playing a cheap Mexican ballad. Lights down to indicate the heavy warmth and thickening glow of midafternoon. Phoebe rolls over, sleeps.*

*Edward enters on tiptoe. Except for his tie, which he has removed, he is dressed as previously. He places three precious sea shells on the table, shakes Phoebe timidly to be certain she is sleeping deeply, looks around to be certain they are alone, finally begins to speak to Phoebe in a voice which suggests stealth, excitement, intimacy.*

EDWARD:

(*leaning close to her*)

Sleeping, Phoebe? I won't disturb you. But now I have you all to myself, all to myself. You and I and the sea shells, Phoebe. I want to show you my sea shells. I've studied them, scrutinized them, catalogued them. The shells come from the sea, but they're really products of my own mind. You have to think about shells to love them.

(*He moves away, rearranges the shells on the table.*)

These rare things, these delicate abstractions of human life, are rock shells, a subfamily of the Murex,

Phoebe. Now, my dear, my princess, the rock shells are distinguished by the striking ornamentation of their whorls by spiny processes. Each varix marks the end of a period of growth, you see, when a barricade is built to guard the temporarily closed doorway. The presence of all these secondary varices is especially significant: it means comparative starvation for the mollusk, which instinctively strengthens the edge of the shell when threatened with, with short rations.
(*He smiles sadly.*)
What I am saying is simply this: that the most gaily decked Murex thus confesses to the greatest struggle for enough to eat.
(*with emphasis*)
Richness of apparel, you see, is really the badge of poverty and privation. We must keep it in mind, Phoebe. We must keep it in mind.
(*He pauses, picks up the first shell.*)
Isn't this beautiful, Phoebe? Isn't it sad? You can see that the Cabbage Murex has a stocky shape, a low spire, a short canal and a swollen body whorl. I can tell you that groups of flat tubercles lie between the varices. But here the mouth is the important thing. And in this shell the mouth (*with emphasis*) is wide and pink-lipped, but orange within. A short canal, a swollen body whorl, an orange mouth—is it a fitting totem for an only daughter, Phoebe? For a young daughter?
(*He pauses, collects himself, picks up the second shell, smiles distantly.*)

The Lurid Murex is pale, reddish yellow to chocolate-colored, sculptured with fine sharp spiral lines and faint rounded varices. These shells are few in number. The specimens are generally worn. What do you think of that, Phoebe? Generally worn. Isn't that a shame?
(*He pauses, picks up the last shell, smiles broadly.*)
Well, here he is, the old Mournful Murex! Yes indeed.
(*His smile fades.*)
The Mournful Murex is dull purplish, you see, with six rusty brown varices spread out and sometimes forming flat, curved spines.
(*Emotionally*)
These are usually broken off.
(*Pause*)
Except near the outer lip. The shoulder of the body whorl bears the largest spines.
(*Pause*)
Well, there we are, and what could be more sad.
(*He laughs.*)
But isn't it a beautiful collection? Isn't it strange? I suppose these are only a few of nature's ornaments gathered by an amateur naturalist. But I wanted you to see them. That is, I—I want you to have them. The Cabbage Murex, the Lurid Murex, the Mournful Murex—they're yours now, Phoebe. Yours to keep. And I hope they affect you as they affect me. My charms, my precious talismans—do you know how they affect me, Phoebe? They make me smile. . . .

(*Edward leaves the shells on the table, happily and stealthily glides upstage and exits.*
*The patio grows silent. After a pause the strains of the Mexican ballad are heard once more.*
*Beatrix enters slowly, obviously straining to achieve as much dignity as possible. Clutching the top of her negligee, she halts upstage, then moves first to the table where she handles the shells, and next to the hammock where she pauses, gathers her strength and, finally, makes a supreme effort to break through the rigid bonds of her reserve into the charm and abandon of the young girl. She opens wide her negligee, revealing an outlandish Victorian undergarment. For a moment her effort to expose a different self is convincing.*)

BEATRIX:
>Look at me, Phoebe. Will you look at me? Oh, laugh if you want to, love, I won't mind. Is all my nakedness amusing? Or is it—is it a precious gift? I'm really not ashamed of my nakedness, Phoebe. Suddenly I'm not at all ashamed. For you I've cast off everything—grief, anger, malice, motherhood, wifehood, a grasping heart—and do you know what I feel like now? I feel like a young girl who walks in the sunlight without her parasol! Do you see it shining in me, Phoebe? The soul of the pretty girl in, in complete submission? I've never been naked like this before—can you believe it?—I've never (*Pause*) gone this far. But then never in my life have I felt so beautifully clothed in modesty. Never, never!

(*She expects but does not receive some sort of response to the joy of her declaration.*)
Phoebe:
(*She leans over the hammock.*)
Don't be afraid, don't be angry, don't be amused....
(*She straightens up, fixes her hair, drops the negligee part way off her shoulders.*)
You do understand me, Phoebe, don't you? You do understand me? I said I would show you my scars, love. Well, here they are. Look at them—my scars, my imperfections—and tell me that you see only the innocent nakedness of the young girl.
(*Pause*)
Phoebe?
(*Again she leans over the hammock.*)
Are you listening?
(*She shakes her.*)
Listen to me, Phoebe....
(*She shakes her violently.*)
Look at me. If you don't you'll be sorry! Phoebe!
(*She grows rigid. Slowly she stands perfectly straight, closes the negligee tightly, clutches it to her throat. Now she speaks with cold vehemence.*)
Scorn? You have only scorn for me? All right. All right.
(*She trembles.*)
Lying there in your, your black brassiere, and marking time with your labored drunken breaths.... You detest me, don't you, Phoebe? Oh, don't fool yourself! I know you detest my age, my vanity, my ignorance of sex; detest the blackness of my tongue,

the circles under my eyes, the furious innocence of my vanity; detest my cold eyes, my flat chest, and most of all the barren condition of my body. You'd hate me for being forty-six years old, Phoebe? You'd hate me for defending my husband and trying to protect my daughter? You'd hate me, would you?
(*She pauses.*)
You devil!

(*In passionate anger she stoops slowly, kisses Phoebe gently. Deliberately she moves to the table, picks up the shells, walks quickly to the pool into which, after a moment's hesitation, she drops the shells. She turns and stares at Phoebe, then exits upstage quickly. The Mexican music swells to almost unbearable volume, abruptly ceases. Lights down further to suggest gathering shadows of a tropical twilight. The silence is broken by subdued incongruous sounds from the radio offstage as Jane switches impatiently from station to station. Jane settles for rock-and-roll, the volume of which increases steadily. Enter Jane, playing an awkward, girlish Caliban, and leaping out of the upstage darkness into the soft light of the patio. Near the pool she cavorts, stumbles, crouches in various animal-like poses. Finally she mimes a happy challenging cry, thumps her naked chest, flings wide her arms, stares rigidly at her aunt asleep in the hammock. Jane, no longer the mere child, walks slowly, silently, ominously to the hammock. She pauses. The radio is silent. Then with extreme and silent vehemence Jane suddenly attacks the sleeping woman, tugs and shakes her, pulls at her head and shoulders as if to drag her from the hammock. She pauses. Then deliberately she seizes the large pocketbook and swings it out of the hammock where it has been partially concealed by Phoebe's body. She backs off and slowly walks upstage center, with the pocketbook dangling from her hand. She is breathing heavily. At last she turns and faces the hammock. Phoebe sits up and stares at her.)*

PHOEBE:
>(*grinning*)
>Hey, mermaid! Baby! What are you doing!

*Lights black out. The rock-and-roll hits a sudden plateau of rapid tempo, intense volume and unvarying pitch. It continues throughout the next scene and, like a stuck record, provides an unrelieved background for the pantomimed action.*

## SCENE 4

*Spotlight stage right on Jane, who is carrying the pocketbook, gently swinging it back and forth. She walks to the end of the diving board, sits and straddles it and hugs the pocketbook while smiling in the direction of the audience. She fondles the hand-tooled leather. Then she opens the pocketbook, extracts from it a handful of bills, which she stuffs around the edge of her bikini, and proceeds to examine the contents of the pocketbook which, item by item, she drops into the pool. Finally she drops the pocketbook itself into the pool, hugs her knees, and continues to smile puckishly at the audience.*

*The spotlight fades. The rock-and-roll dissolves slowly to static, which fades to silence. Then from the radio offstage comes the sound of dinner music, scratchy and long out of date.*

## SCENE 5

*Lights up softly stage left on Phoebe, Edward and Beatrix at dinner. They are midway through the meal and obviously have been eating in strained silence. It is well into the night, the table is lavishly set, already the candles are burning low. Throughout the scene Phoebe, who is now wearing her skin-tight, silver lamé evening gown, drinks tequila steadily and attempts to force it on Edward and Beatrix.*

PHOEBE:
> Where's Jane?

EDWARD:
> She says she has a pain in her stomach.

PHOEBE:
> I'm sure she does.

BEATRIX:
> She says she's not feeling well.

PHOEBE:
> I'm sure she's not.

BEATRIX:
> She's nauseous.

EDWARD:
> I think you should take her temperature, Beatrix.

PHOEBE:
> Good idea. But after dessert.

**EDWARD:**
>Yes. I think you should wait until after dessert, Beatrix.
>(*Pause*)

**PHOEBE:**
>She's sick a lot? Always complaining of these mysterious pains in her stomach?

**EDWARD:**
>She's a sturdy youngster.

**BEATRIX:**
>It's not at all like Jane to have intestinal trouble.

**PHOEBE:**
>Well, she's missing a good meal. Too bad.

**EDWARD:**
>Save something for her, Beatrix.

**PHOEBE:**
>Take Jane's plate to her room later. Maybe she'll choke down a few mouthfuls.
>(*Pause*)
>How's her head?

**BEATRIX:**
>She says her head hurts also.

**EDWARD:**
>I wish she'd stop listening to that radio. No wonder she has a headache.

(*Phoebe laughs.*)

**BEATRIX:**
>It's not the radio.

PHOEBE:
> (*laughing*)
> Where is the pain exactly, baby? It's just possible she's got appendicitis.

EDWARD:
> Do you think so, Beatrix?

BEATRIX:
> No. It isn't appendicitis.

PHOEBE:
> Well, I wish I had your confidence, baby. I wish I. . . .

EDWARD:
> Phoebe? We're sorry, Phoebe.

PHOEBE:
> What do you mean, sorry? Janie's sick, she's sick. It's not your fault.

BEATRIX:
> It's our fault. We're responsible.

PHOEBE:
> Don't worry, don't worry. . . . We'll give her a shot of tequila if she doesn't snap out of it. Drink up, you two.

(*Pause. Edward and Beatrix pick at their food, refuse to drink.*)

EDWARD:
> Phoebe?

PHOEBE:
> Baby?

EDWARD:

>(*changing his mind*)
>Have some more country ham, Phoebe.
>(*Pause*)

PHOEBE:

>There's always the risk of appendicitis. If the tequila doesn't do the trick I'll find a telephone somewhere and call an ambulance.

BEATRIX:

>That's won't be necessary.

PHOEBE:

>In a case like this, baby, who knows?

BEATRIX:

>Phoebe, please. . . .

PHOEBE:

>Can you imagine an ambulance in here? The long white emergency arm of medical science in the Garden of Eden. . . . Interns in white uniforms fighting their way through the orchids. . . . Janie would love that.

BEATRIX:

>It's not paradise. Believe me.

PHOEBE:

>You think it's not? Orchids, bougainvillea, acacia trees, all these doves and the swamp moss like frozen mist—lots of people would call it paradise.

BEATRIX:

>This place? Look around you, Phoebe. Look around

you at desolation. No electricity, no water in the swimming pool, no telephone....

EDWARD:

She's right, Phoebe. The lines are down.

BEATRIX:

Dust and weeds and rampant jungle and rotting mattresses in empty rooms. There aren't even any screens on the windows. Someone slashed all the screens on the windows. With a knife....

PHOEBE:

An inexpensive retreat amidst luxuriant growth, baby. What more do you want? It's beautiful.

BEATRIX:

An abandoned motel on the edge of the universe. It smells of obsolescence and rank decay, it smells of the tears of uncouth strangers and the refuse of their sordid pleasures. It smells of death. Is this any kind of home for me? Is this any kind of home for a growing girl?

PHOEBE:

You're hard to please.

BEATRIX:

I always wanted to grow old in Santa Barbara, Phoebe. I wanted to die in comfort.

PHOEBE:

You're better off here. You don't suffer any hardships here.

**BEATRIX:**
> Edward! Tell her, tell her. Tell Phoebe about the centipede!

**EDWARD:**
> It's unimportant. We won't burden Phoebe with our trivial discomforts.

**BEATRIX:**
> Tell her. Tell her. I insist she know the facts of our existence.

**EDWARD:**
> Please. It's only a centipede, Beatrix.

**BEATRIX:**
> Only a centipede! Only the sting of death. . . .
> (*to Phoebe*)
> In all your travels, have you ever actually seen a centipede? Have you?

**PHOEBE:**
> (*laughing*)
> I've seen everything else. Spiders in Mexico, hooded cobras in India, rats on the banks of the Seine, black panthers stalking on the tops of city walls in North Africa. These things don't bother me, baby.

**BEATRIX:**
> No, no, they wouldn't bother you, Phoebe.

**EDWARD:**
> She was always so headstrong, so daring, Beatrix, wasn't she. . . .

BEATRIX:

> But Edward has to shave. Poor Edward has to shave. And he doesn't have an electric razor, Phoebe.

PHOEBE:

> Jane was supposed to bring back some blades with the supplies. What more do you want?

BEATRIX:

> Nothing, love, nothing at all. . . . But every morning poor Edward has to shave. Every morning in his transparent undershirt and trousers—they're old, Phoebe, you can see through them, as you know—every morning Edward stands on the broken tiles in front of the cracked and rusty sink and tries to shave. I assist him. I hold the towel. The sink is bloodstained. Yes, bloodstained. They used to commit murders in this motel.

(*Phoebe laughs. For the balance of the scene Edward and Beatrix neither eat nor drink.*)

> Go ahead, Phoebe. Laugh. I expect you to laugh.

PHOEBE:

> Is he an invalid?
> (*She laughs again, takes a long drink of tequila.*)
> Is he some kind of poor paralytic son-of-a-bitch who has to have a nurse when he shaves?

BEATRIX:

> (*standing and knocking over a glass*)
> I forbid your foul language! Do you hear me?

**EDWARD:**
>(*coaxing Beatrix back into her chair*)
>It's all right, it's all right, my dear. Phoebe may talk as she wishes. She means no harm.

**PHOEBE:**
>Quite true, baby. I mean no harm.

**BEATRIX:**
>Please keep this in mind: I am a good mother. I am a good wife. I am not a—not a nurse, Phoebe.

**EDWARD:**
>Of course you're not. You're a lovely woman. I'm proud of you....

**PHOEBE:**
>She's a lurid—lurid something or other. That's what she is. And let's keep this in mind: in one of those back rooms you've got a fifteen-year-old daughter sick with a bellyache. So sick she won't even show her face. Let's keep it in mind.
>(*Pause. Phoebe drinks.*)

**EDWARD:**
>I shave in tepid water. We've given up trying to warm it, haven't we.
>(*He smiles.*)

**BEATRIX:**
>Yes, in tepid water.

**EDWARD:**
>It's not good for the skin.

PHOEBE:
> Try a new blade next time, baby. It'll help.

BEATRIX:
> (*slowly*)
> Every morning Edward and I go into that filthy little bathroom, he with his razor, I with the towel, and we stand there waiting for the centipede. Tell her, Edward.

EDWARD:
> We don't exactly wait for it. Do we, Beatrix?

(*Phoebe laughs.*)

BEATRIX:
> We wait for it. We anticipate it. Every morning, faithfully, we try to begin the new day, Edward and I, while Jane stumbles out here to the patio nearly naked and rubbing her eyes. Jane won't even brush her hair, Phoebe, she's a rebellious child. But Edward and I still fight for our old lives. . . .

EDWARD:
> Of course we do. . . .

BEATRIX:
> Fight, yes, fight for our lives. So Edward shaves. We look at each other, we try to smile, the sun burns through a crack in the concrete—there's grass growing in the shower stall, Phoebe, crab grass!—and Edward tightens the dull blade in his safety razor and leans over the sink. It's dawn, and

we wait in silence, two old people trying to begin the day. Then Edward reaches for the faucet, and the first trickle of tepid water must wake it up, because that's the moment the centipede leaps up at us! One minute there's nothing but water trickling down the drain, and the next minute there's the centipede jumping at us, shooting up out of the little rusty drainhole in the bottom of the basin like a monster! That's when I scream! Yes, Phoebe, scream, scream! Because the centipede is as long as my hand and as big around as my thumb, a slick wriggling monster like a giant worm with a hundred little thrashing legs and horns on one end and a forked tail at the other, a wet brown worm with yellow spots and enough poison in its forked tail to kill us both!

**EDWARD:**

Poor Beatrix....

**BEATRIX:**

It jumps and wriggles and races around the rim of the basin until I go into action. Yes, Phoebe, it's up to me, since your brother is helpless before the centipede and can only smile, while Jane doesn't know or care what's happening to us in the bathroom every morning. And do you know how I vanquish the centipede? I stoop and reach for the coffee can under the sink and I catch the centipede in the can and take it outside and fling it away, fling it as far as I can into the festering swamp. Then I rejoin Edward, who shaves in peace.

EDWARD:
>Isn't she wonderful?

BEATRIX:
>Could you do it, Phoebe? Could you live this way?

EDWARD:
>But isn't it strange that the centipede always returns to our bathroom drain?

BEATRIX:
>Yes. Day after day it returns. I'm not afraid for Edward and myself. But I'm afraid for Jane. What if the centipede comes out of the drain some night, Phoebe, and stings Jane in her sleep? I live in fear of that moment.

PHOEBE:
>(*laughing*)
>Good for the centipede. Maybe tonight it'll get all three of you.
>(*She drinks.*)

BEATRIX:
>You don't mean that.

PHOEBE:
>Don't I?

EDWARD:
>(*smiling*)
>I didn't shave this morning. For your sake we didn't want to risk the noise.
>(*Pause*)

BEATRIX:
> Well? What do you think of our paradise now, Phoebe? Is this your idea of Eden? Is this where you want your brother and sister-in-law and little niece to live? Can you bear to see us amidst all this disrepair and this—this degradation, Phoebe?

PHOEBE:
> It's all in your head. You've got a head full of degradation, that's the trouble. It flows like sap from a dead tree.

BEATRIX:
> Revile me, Phoebe. Go on, revile me.

PHOEBE:
> I haven't begun.
> (*She drinks.*)

EDWARD:
> What about your suitcases, Phoebe? We should get the rest of your bags out of the car, shouldn't we?

(*Phoebe laughs.*)

BEATRIX:
> So it's all in my head. All this collapse and ruin and ignominy is my invention, is that it?

PHOEBE:
> That's it.

BEATRIX:
> To you I'm just an hysterical woman who spends her time inventing lies and complaining in the midst of plenty?

PHOEBE:
> Bitching—bitching long and loud in the lap of luxury.

EDWARD:
> Phoebe, please. . . . Let's get the bags.

BEATRIX:
> So you don't believe our ignominy. . . .

PHOEBE:
> No. I don't believe it.

BEATRIX:
> And you detest me, Phoebe. Is that it?

PHOEBE:
> (*laughing*)
> Drink up, you prudes. I didn't bring all this tequila from Tequila for nothing.

(*She drinks. Edward and Beatrix sit facing her like ghosts.*)

BEATRIX:
> It's not fair! It's not just!
> (*She stands again, knocks over another glass.*)
> Do you know what Jane found the first day we came to this—this place?

EDWARD:
> Wait, Beatrix, please. . . .

BEATRIX:
> She found a sign. That's right, a sign! It was half buried at the edge of the swamp, and she was just a

little girl. But she dragged it out. An old wooden sign with three words painted on it in fading letters and nearly obliterated by innumerable tiny holes....

EDWARD:

(*softly*)
Shotgun blasts.... Those holes were from shotgun blasts, my dear.

BEATRIX:

Do you know what was painted on that sign, Phoebe? Do you?
(*She pauses breathlessly, slowly regains her strength and rigid control.*)
I'll tell you, Phoebe. COLORED ONLY. VACANCY. That's what was painted on our sign!

PHOEBE:

(*laughing*)
You came to the right place ...!

BEATRIX:

(*shaking off Edward, who has been trying to coax her to sit down again*)
A bullet-riddled sign, Phoebe. Is that my invention too? Is it? Jane's got that sign on the wall of her room. You can look at it for yourself. Go, go, Phoebe, look for yourself ...!

(*Phoebe stands, doubles up drunkenly with laughter.*)

Laugh, laugh! But it's not my invention. I swear it's not. Listen to the words, you pitiless woman: COLORED ONLY. VACANCY. Is that ignominy, Phoebe?

COLORED, COLORED, COLORED ONLY! That's what I call ignominy, Phoebe. Ignominy and disgrace and degradation!

(*Phoebe, still laughing, tries to reach out her arm toward Beatrix.*)

Don't touch me, Phoebe. I'm warning you. . . .

EDWARD:
Phoebe. Sit down. Please.

(*Phoebe collapses in her chair.*)

BEATRIX:
(*triumphantly*)
Now do you believe me? Will you take my word for it that this place is cursed and rotten and filthy? Is it what we deserve, Phoebe? Tell me honestly!

PHOEBE:
(*still laughing*)
Yes. . . . Yes, it's what you deserve. . . . Exactly. . . . My God, you came to the right place. . . . Wonderful, wonderful . . . !

BEATRIX:
You dare!

EDWARD:
Take a drink of your—your tequila, Phoebe. Please.
(*to Beatrix*)
She's going to choke, do something. . . .

BEATRIX:
You devil! You fiend!

(*She flings a glass of water in Phoebe's face, stands trembling and watching in fury as Phoebe gasps, laughs fitfully, slowly wipes her face with a napkin.*)

PHOEBE:

    It's the right place, all right. . . . My God, my God. . . . How perfect.
(*collecting herself*)
Twenty years, you two, just think of it. Twenty years of laws as long as your arm and—and shotguns for shooting holes in signs, and everybody trying to learn just one chorus of one Negro spiritual and raising hell and trying to find just one bowl, one pot to hold all the blood and water and wash off all the crap in; twenty years of pain and violence and fund drives and—and *civil disobedience*, by God; twenty years of everybody worrying and working their heads off and passing laws and gouging flesh and floundering in the River of Jordan and making a little progress—we'll drink to that—and then the three of you end up in the ruins of a segregated motel! There's justice for you! There's a fitting end for you! All three of you dreaming or bitching away in this stinking place—this beautifully stinking place—and you can't even see the humor of it. My God!

BEATRIX:

    I've had enough.

PHOEBE:

    I'll bet you have.

**BEATRIX:**
> Enough. Enough.

(*She turns, stumbles, walks off slowly into the darkness upstage. Edward attempts to straighten china and glassware, to clear a path across the table between himself and Phoebe, while Phoebe laboriously takes another drink.*)

**EDWARD:**
> I'm sorry.

**PHOEBE:**
> Don't apologize.

**EDWARD:**
> She's high-strung.

**PHOEBE:**
> That's right.

**EDWARD:**
> Yes. I'm afraid she's very high-strung at times.

**PHOEBE:**
> You don't need to explain.

**EDWARD:**
> She's strong. Beatrix is a very strong woman, Phoebe. But she trembles. I hate to see Beatrix trembling.

**PHOEBE:**
> So do I.

**EDWARD:**
> I hate to see her whole life (*Pause*) vibrating that way.

PHOEBE:

>It's pathetic.

EDWARD:

>But she didn't mean all those things she said tonight.

PHOEBE:

>Forget it. For your sake and mine, forget it.

EDWARD:

>She wasn't herself tonight, Phoebe. Was she?

PHOEBE:

>She was herself all right. Beatrix at her best.

EDWARD:

>She was trembling. She didn't mean all those cruel things she said.

PHOEBE:

>You know what's the matter with her? She's got a black tongue. Yes, a black tongue, baby. Take my word for it.

EDWARD:

>Phoebe—a little more ham, Phoebe? Have another drink of—of tequila.

PHOEBE:

>I've had enough.
>(*She takes a quick gulp from her glass.*)

EDWARD:

>Forgive her. Won't you? The trouble tonight was Jane. She was thinking of Jane.

PHOEBE:

>Look. I don't want to hear that name.

EDWARD:

>A daughter of ours, Phoebe. We can't understand it. We don't understand how it happened.

PHOEBE:

>What the hell have you been teaching her all these years?

EDWARD:

>I don't know, I don't know. I wish I knew.

PHOEBE:

>It must have been something to write home to the girls about. But I'll tell you this: it's too late now.

EDWARD:

>Please don't say it's too late. Please. . . .

PHOEBE:

>The damage is done. I'm sick of the whole thing.

EDWARD:

>Give her another chance. What happened this afternoon was an accident. We're so ashamed. . . .

PHOEBE:

>You know as well as I do it was deliberate.

EDWARD:

>Phoebe, please. . . .

PHOEBE:

>I was sleeping. Jane saw her chance. It's simple.

EDWARD:

    Forgive her, Phoebe. Forgive Beatrix and me.

PHOEBE:

    Simple, simple, I tell you.
    (*Pause*)
    Did you two prudes put her up to it?

EDWARD:

    (*standing*)
    Let's get your bags out of the car. Right now, Phoebe. You can't go on living out of a single suitcase.... We're so ashamed.

PHOEBE:

    She stole from me. You hear that? She stole from her own flesh and blood. My God.

(*She drinks. Edward steps toward her.*)

EDWARD:

    Phoebe? We need you, Phoebe....

PHOEBE:

    Am I hearing things?

EDWARD:

    Beatrix needs medical attention, Jane needs education, I'd like to open this motel. Wouldn't I make a good manager of a motel, Phoebe?

PHOEBE:

    I'm hearing things. My God!

EDWARD:

    Help us. Will you help us?

(*They stare at each other. Phoebe grins, slowly raises her glass at arm's length as if to toast her brother.*)

PHOEBE:
> Tell Jane to come out here. I want to talk to Jane. Alone.

*Edward smiles hopefully, backs away while making delicate placating gestures with his hands, turns and exits into the darkness upstage. Phoebe continues to hold her glass as in a toast. After a pause the dinner music offstage switches abruptly to futuristic rock-and-roll.*

# SCENE 6

*Jane enters, carrying the radio which increases slightly in volume as she comes in. Grinning and moving with awkward assurance, she walks directly to the pool, peers into it, glances boldly over her shoulder at Phoebe. Then she circles the table, inspects the wreckage of the meal, finally leans on the edge of the table, crosses her legs, stares down with arrogant good humor at Phoebe.*

**PHOEBE:**
> (*abruptly, softly, still holding out the glass*)
> Hey, mermaid! Hey, baby! What are you staring at?

**JANE:**
> It's a swell night.

**PHOEBE:**
> It's a swell party.

**JANE:**
> (*with pleasure*)
> You want some company?

(*Phoebe rises slowly, unsteadily.*)

**PHOEBE:**
> Here's to you, baby. To you and me. And to a long night of—of insurrection!

(*With a slow theatrical flourish Phoebe completes the toast, drinks down the tequila remaining in her glass.*

*Phoebe and Jane laugh. And suddenly, as by prearranged signal, they gather up two bottles, two glasses, the candles, and quickly move stage right where Phoebe sits on the edge of the pool and Jane sits on the leg rest of the deck chair. Phoebe fills the glasses. Moonlight and candlelight illumine the pair.)*

JANE:

Well, here's to us!

PHOEBE:

Drink up, baby.

JANE:

(*taking her first sip of tequila*)
Wow!

PHOEBE:

That's the spirit.

(*Jane drinks again.*)

JANE:

Wow! I'm reeling!

PHOEBE:

Feeling warm, baby?

JANE:

It makes you sweat!

PHOEBE:

You've got the moon in your eyes, baby. Keep going.

JANE:

I'm on cloud nine already.

**PHOEBE:**
>That's the spirit.

(*Jane drinks.*)

**JANE:**
>Say, I'll bet *he* didn't try this stuff.

**PHOEBE:**
>He'd choke on it.

**JANE:**
>He's not a sport like you.

**PHOEBE:**
>Give him a sea shell, baby, and he's pleased as punch.

**JANE:**
>(*mimicking Edward*)
>In the Murex the sexes are distinct!

(*They laugh.*)

**PHOEBE:**
>You were born from a little barnacle, did you know that?

**JANE:**
>Some barnacle!

(*They laugh. Jane drinks.*)

**PHOEBE:**
>Your mother objects to my tequila.

**JANE:**
>If she put this glass to her mouth she'd go up in smoke!

PHOEBE:

Black smoke.

JANE:

Beatrix in her burning girdle!

PHOEBE:

That's the spirit.

(*They drink.*)

JANE:

You know what time they go to bed? Nine o'clock! They make me go to bed at nine o'clock!

PHOEBE:

Baby, from now on you can stay up all night if you want to.

JANE:

I've got to start living some time.

PHOEBE:

We'll live together. We'll hit the bottle together every night.
(*Pause*)
Can you dance, baby? I'll teach you to dance.

JANE:

I can't dance.

PHOEBE:

You've got to shake it, baby. I'll show you how.

JANE:

(*drinking*)
I can't dance. They don't want me to dance. They

don't want me listening to the Sting Rays, they don't want me listening to *Comic Strip of the Air*, they don't want me looking at nudie magazines or *Body Science*. They won't let me read *The Naked Family*, they won't send me away to health camp, they won't let me swim, they won't even let me breathe. They're trying to—trying to stifle me! They don't want me to mature!

PHOEBE:

You'll mature all right. Don't worry.

JANE:

They're trying to starve me to death. They're trying to kill my mind!

PHOEBE:

Baby, baby, don't worry about it.

JANE:

They're trying to shrink my bosom! They don't want me to have a bosom!

PHOEBE:

Is that any way for a mermaid to talk?

JANE:

I'm full of despair, I tell you.

PHOEBE:

Listen, baby, everything's going to be different. We're going to dance and drink tequila and go for three A.M. rides in the white Caddy. We're going to pick up some boys and drive away at a hundred miles an hour, did you know that?

JANE:
> (*sullenly, taking another drink*)
> What about my bosom?

PHOEBE:
> (*laughing*)
> You don't have to worry about your physique, with me around.

JANE:
> (*sullenly*)
> I've got to start living some time.

PHOEBE:
> I'll breathe a little life into you, don't worry.

JANE:
> Is that a promise?

PHOEBE:
> Sure, sure it is. A promise.

JANE:
> Well, then, here's to us.

PHOEBE:
> To you and me!

(*They drink.*)

JANE:
> Phoebe—you're not angry?

PHOEBE:
> Why, baby? Is something wrong?

JANE:

> *You* know, Phoebe.
> (*She drinks.*)
> And you're not angry? Really?

PHOEBE:

> Baby, you know the score. So let's get down to business.

JANE:

> I don't know what you're talking about.

PHOEBE:

> We're going to dance—remember?

JANE:

> Dance by yourself. I'm working on this tequila.
> (*She drinks.*)
> Wow!

PHOEBE:

> Look at those legs. Look at your eyes and mouth and hair. Look at your body. But we've got to liberate you, we've got to find the rhythm. You've got to stand up here and shake it. Right now.

JANE:

> (*gulping the tequila*)
> Count me out. I'm drinking.

PHOEBE:

> The bongo drums, baby—don't you hear them?

JANE:

> Leave me alone. I can't dance.

PHOEBE:
> The moon, the music, the beat, the hot night air, the two of us—don't you want to learn to dance? Don't you want to dance with your old Phoebe?

JANE:
> But I can't even move! I'm reeling!

PHOEBE:
> No more stalling, baby. On your feet!

(*They struggle and pull each other upright.*)

JANE:
> Wow! I'm reeling!

PHOEBE:
> That's the spirit!

(*They click glasses and drink. The rock-and-roll grows louder.*)

JANE:
> (*laughing, swaying*)
> What are we doing? I can't feel a thing. I'm numb.

(*Phoebe leans forward at an awkward angle, carefully places the flat of her hand on Jane's thigh.*)

PHOEBE:
> How about that? Do you feel that?

JANE:
> I don't feel a thing. What is it?

PHOEBE:
> My hand, just my guiding hand.

(*She laughs, begins to slap Jane's thigh in time to the music.*)
Do you feel it now? Wake up, baby, open your senses, let your flesh slide away from you and your skin tingle, let your sweet self respond, baby, because I'm beating the rhythm of life into you with my bare hand.... Don't you feel it?

JANE:

I don't feel it.
(*Pause*)
But take your hand off me, Phoebe. Leave me alone.

(*Phoebe steps back quickly, laughs, glances at Jane, drinks.*)

PHOEBE:

This is no time to be like your mother, baby. I'm going to excite you, baby—do you hear me?—you're going to dance!

JANE:

I'm drinking tequila. I'm probably (*proudly*) comatose already!
(*She drinks.*)
Wow! I'm lucky not to be flat on my face.

PHOEBE:

Concentrate, baby. Limber up. You've got to try, baby, please.... You've got to do what I say.

JANE:

I can't move. I don't know how. I'm innocent, I'm hopeless, I don't know which way to turn.

*(She laughs, throws back her head and drinks.)*
I don't know the proper steps!

**PHOEBE:**

You're stalling. You're holding out on me.

**JANE:**

I'm young and innocent. I'm clumsy on my feet.

**PHOEBE:**

Let go, baby. Let go!

**JANE:**

I don't know how to begin, I tell you.
*(She drinks.)*
I don't know how to shake it, my mind's a blank.
*(Pause)*

**PHOEBE:**

All right, all right. Watch me.
*(Phoebe sets down her glass, gathers high the tight silver skirt of her evening gown, and with increasingly strenuous effort and excitement improvises a dance. She strains to talk above the music which swells to her physical exertions and underlying fatigue.)*
You've got to rumble, see . . . ? You grunt with your knees and elbows, you pace out your breath and hum with your mind. . . . It's easy. . . . You just —just hang yourself in the air. . . . You sweat in the shadow of a crazy boy. . . . It's easy. . . .

**JANE:**

*(drinking and laughing)*
Shake it, Phoebe!

**PHOEBE:**

(*still dancing, greatly encouraged*)
Down there in your knees and legs and fanny you're furious. . . . But your face . . . . is full of joy. . . . You probe the music with your face. . . . You rock. . . . Like this, see . . . ? Steady pressure. . . . Hummingbirds flying out of your open mouth and your eyes half shut. . . . Your boyfriend is snapping his fingers . . . . twitching his lips. . . . There's no contact. . . . But then . . . . suddenly you feel his finger on the last node of your spine. . . . He pushes the button. . . . The bell rings. . . .

**JANE:**

Jump, Phoebe, jump!

**PHOEBE:**

(*still dancing*)
Use your feet. Don't be afraid to use your feet. . . . Like this. . . . Your boyfriend has the most beautiful black leather pants in the world. . . . You keep your eye on them, baby. . . . He's laughing. . . . So . . . . you rub the air with—with everything you've got. . . . And you've got a night-blooming cereus full of agony, baby. . . . But it's wonderful . . . . wonderful. . . .

**JANE:**

(*laughing*)
Look out, Phoebe. You'll kill yourself.

**PHOEBE:**

(*bewildered, slowly ceasing her dance*)
Kill myself? Don't you worry, baby. I'm a practiced dancer.

*(She falls to her knees at Jane's feet, picks up her glass and drinks.)*

JANE:
You're great! Phoebe the savage dancer!

PHOEBE:
*(panting)*
Sure I'm great, baby. You get the idea? It's easy.

JANE:
I get the idea.

PHOEBE:
*(dropping her glass, throwing her arms around Jane)*
Come on then, try it yourself.

JANE:
Hey, hands off!

PHOEBE:
*(holding Jane and hauling herself to her feet)*
Come on, come on, we'll slobber all over each other, baby! We'll glow together....

JANE:
Not a chance!

PHOEBE:
*(disregarding Jane and trying to manipulate Jane's body as she talks)*
Raise your arms, bend your knees, let your shoulders go, flex your belly—come on, flex it—put some bounce in your fanny....

*(They struggle.)*

Swim to me, baby. Don't be afraid....

JANE:

    (*laughing, pushing Phoebe away*)
I'm not afraid. But get off me, get away!

PHOEBE:

    (*panting, trying to smile*)
Come on, baby, you can do it. I know you can do it. Please. . . .

JANE:

    I don't want to do it.

PHOEBE:

    See? It's easy.
(*She smiles, feebly tries again to pose as the dancer.*)
See? You're athletic, you're full of life, you're free. I need you, baby. We'll listen to the Sting Rays together. We'll read *The Naked Family*. I know the taste of your blood, baby. I even know the color of your breath. It's pale blue. Compassion, tingling tenderness, the road of life—come on, baby, swim to me . . . . you baby shark. . . .

JANE:

    You're drunk. You better cool off, Phoebe, before you break a blood vessel or something.

PHOEBE:

    What are you saying . . . .

JANE:

    I don't want you around my pool. I don't want any part of you. Now sack out in your hammock, Phoebe, before I yell for Dad!

(*They stare at each other. Then Phoebe, swaying slightly, smiles with tenderness and affection at Jane and slowly kneels, blows out the candles, seizes one of the tequila bottles by the neck. Then she rises, staggers to center stage and faces up into the darkness. The rock-and-roll plays softly and steadily on.*)

PHOEBE:

    (*loudly, releasing her grief and anger*)
Listen to me, you two. Sit up in there, you two—you weak sisters, you little children lost in the woods. Hug each other and listen to me, hear old Phoebe roar!
(*She drinks from the bottle.*)
Look what you've done to her, look what you've done to my baby, my poor Jane. You with your grasping hearts, you with your—your pee-pot morality! Jane says I'm drunk . . . . (*She drinks.*) so I must be drunk. And I'm rich and I'm beautiful and I'm lascivious and I'm selfish. But look what you've done to Jane—you've crippled her! Look at what you've brought into the world, look at your spawn. A thief, you hear? A thief who deals from her own flesh and blood! Taste the ashes of your dead Sunday schools, you two—Jane will destroy you yet, she'll destroy your relentless faces and your frightened eyes. Yes, yes, she'll swallow your frightened eyeballs whole. (*She drinks.*) You hear me in there? You're nothing but a couple of sea shells that mated by accident long ago in warm water. You Mournful Murex! You—you Lurid Murex! Nothing but a

couple of dead Christians from the faded white time of pee-pot morality. (*She drinks.*) Well, the hell with you! The hell with you both and your pride and your pleas for help. I'm going back for a little trip on the *Santa Maria*. I've got the fare! But you better listen to me, you two—can you hear me in there? Watch out, you two. Watch out for the centipede. He bites!

(*Phoebe takes a step, slowly collapses, falls unconscious in the darkness. Jane waits, then crosses and kneels at her side. The music rises toward a crescendo, slowly fades. Edward and Beatrix enter together on tiptoe upstage center. Only their faces, lit by the candles they carry, are seen.*)

BEATRIX:
    Jane?

EDWARD:
    Phoebe?

BEATRIX:
    What is she doing to you, Jane?

EDWARD:
    Do you need me, Jane? Are you all right?

BEATRIX:
    Oh, the fiend! The fiend!

(*Jane lifts her head slowly.*)

JANE:
    Get out. Get out of here. Go back to sleep.

(*softly*)
She's mine, all mine. I'll take care of her.

*The candles are extinguished as by a sudden breath of fresh air. Beatrix and Edward exit.*
*Jane rises, looks around her, with sudden purpose crosses to the radio, turns it to full volume, collects herself. Then, under spotlight and smiling with joy, she begins to dance, powerfully and with great skill and grace. At the height of Jane's dance the overpowering sound of water rushing into the swimming pool fills the stage and obliterates the music.*
*As Jane begins to dance toward the upstage exit the roar of the water diminishes to a lapping and trickling sound, while the spotlight fades into the rising glow of dawn. Jane exits upstage, the hammock and Phoebe's suitcase are gone.*

## SCENE 7

*Silence. The warm light of dawn grows more intense. Jane enters, pauses upstage, then slowly approaching the pool she pantomimes each of the actions she describes.*

JANE:

Listen, Phoebe, I'm trying to tell you something. I come out here every morning, before it's light. I stand here and I touch myself—on the arms, the legs—touch myself like this a few times even though it's always hot from yesterday. Then I told my hand in front of my face until I see it. Then I sniff because I want to know if I can smell the flowers. Then I listen, and I think I'll hear it trickling, or I think I'll hear drops of it dripping at the edge, and I think of fish and whales and seaweed and big jelly fish sitting like eggs without shells in pools of clear water. I listen and don't hear anything but doves. Still I think it's filling up—maybe this time it's already reached the top—and I start walking over to it. And then, listening and holding my breath, Phoebe, I kneel down at the edge.
(*She kneels and smiles at the audience.*)
Then I look.
(*She does not look into the pool, but rather continues to smile at the audience.*)
I look into the swimming pool and try to see our faces in the water.

*Lights fade quickly to black.*

## CURTAIN

# THE WAX MUSEUM

The Wax Museum *was first performed by the Theater Company of Boston on April 28, 1966, under the direction of David Wheeler. Bingo was played by Naomi Thornton and Sally Ann was played by Blythe Danner.*

*The interior of a wax museum in a small Canadian beach resort in early summer. The set is dominated by George, a life-sized figure of a Royal Canadian Mounted Policeman who, in full dress uniform (crimson tunic, wide-brimmed hat, riding boots, etc.), stands at attention near the wall at stage right. He is an old dummy, picked and poked at by the public; his face is set in an absurdly happy and boyish smile. Against the wall near George is a small plush-covered bench. Bulky shapes upstage and stage left suggest waxen figures of Queen Elizabeth and Prince Philip, Sir Winston Churchill, the Duke and Duchess of Windsor, Cleopatra, Sherlock Holmes, Lord Nelson dying on the deck of his ship. The room is full of shadows cast by irregular emanations of lurid light.*

BINGO. *The young attendant in the wax museum. She is pretty, sexually aggressive, lively of spirit. With her bright waxen complexion and wearing her uniform (an ill-fitting, shabby crimson tunic and brown skirt), she might be one of the historical figures come to life. Her only passion is George, whom she caresses constantly.*

SALLY ANN. *The virgin. She wears a hat, ill-fitting brown traveling suit, stockings, and on her bosom an orchid. She carries a pocketbook on a strap over her shoulder.*

FRANK. *Her fiancé. He appears only as an offstage voice at the end of the play.*

*Lights up slowly on George and Bingo, who stands frozen with her arm around the dummy and her head on his chest. She is smiling. In the darkness upstage Sally Ann moves to and fro inspecting the wax figures. She is distracted, agitated. She moves downstage, crosses to George and Bingo, stares at them, wheels and darts upstage. Slowly Bingo comes to life, separates herself from George, straightens her tunic, smooths the dummy's chest and grins up at him.*

BINGO:
> Come off it, George. Come off it.
> (*She backs away, puts her hands on her hips, shakes her head, then laughs, steps close to him again.*)
> Just look at you. Pocket open (*She opens it.*), collar undone (*She unfastens it.*), hat on the back of your head (*She tilts the hat.*)—you're a messy chap, George! Unfit for the service! What will the customers think, my boy?
> (*She raps him on the chest, shakes her head in mock despondency.*)
> Not worth the price of a ticket—a bloody disgrace —just shows what the country's coming to—even the Mounties have gone downhill.
> (*She raps him again.*)
> You're immoral, Georgie, that's what!
> (*She stares up into his smiling face, speaks warmly.*)
> You're not respectable. That's what. You're not nice to girls. But you better return to the straight and narrow . . . .

(*Her hands creep up his chest, reach his shoulders, stop short of an embrace.*)
or you can just give me back my photograph. You've got my body but not my soul....
(*Her face is radiant, she shudders.*)
and you won't have my body for long if you don't watch yourself. Do you hear, George?
(*Now she speaks with pure adoration.*)
No more loving, my boy, unless you comb your hair and pull yourself together and obey orders and leave the girls alone and go out there and get your man.
(*She laughs, holds herself at arm's length from him, opens the top button of his tunic.*)
You better watch yourself, my boy, I'm not going to throw my life away on a broken-down old Mountie without principles. The customers wouldn't approve, would they, George.
(*She tears her hands away from him, turns, tries to collect herself, notices Sally Ann and speaks to her sharply.*)
Don't touch the living statues, miss. *If* you don't mind.

SALLY ANN:
Oh I wasn't touching them.

BINGO:
You were feeling the side of Winnie's face. I saw.

SALLY ANN:
Oh no, you're wrong. I....

THE WAX MUSEUM

BINGO:
> You were running your fingernail down Winnie's cheek. That wasn't nice.

SALLY ANN:
> But I wouldn't do such a thing. I wouldn't. And anyway I was standing by Sherlock Holmes, not Winston Churchill.

BINGO:
> Poor Winnie. Everybody wants to scratch his jowls.

SALLY ANN:
> I haven't done anything wrong. And I can tell a famous detective from a—from a wonderful old prime minister.

BINGO:
> The wax is poison.

SALLY ANN:
> What?

BINGO:
> That's right. Deadly poison.

(*Sally Ann takes a few steps toward Bingo, stares down at her hands.*)

> Deadly. It produces fever, a rash as red as strawberries, and blindness. It affects childbearing too. Little newborn babies come out looking like little transparent corkscrews.

(*Sally Ann starts back.*)

> But I see you're not pregnant. You're lucky.

SALLY ANN:
> I only wanted to know was it hard or soft.

BINGO:
> God, the curiosity of people off the streets. . . .

SALLY ANN:
> And did it feel anything like skin.

BINGO:
> Well, did it?

SALLY ANN:
> Yes.

BINGO:
> Well, what did you expect?

SALLY ANN:
> It felt like—like velvet.

BINGO:
> Now you've had a feel of poor old Winnie I hope it was worth it. Couldn't you read the signs? They've got signs all over the place: DO NOT TOUCH THE WAX. Good thing you're not pregnant.

SALLY ANN:
> (*stepping close to Bingo, whispering*)
> I thought you were one.

BINGO:
> One what?

SALLY ANN:
> (*gesturing, mildly frightened*)
> One of them. A dummy.

(*She points to George.*)
Like him. Only a girl.

BINGO:

(*to George*)
Well how about that, Georgie. Shall I slap her face?

SALLY ANN:

Please, I didn't mean to say anything wrong.

BINGO:

You better watch out who you call a dummy.

SALLY ANN:

Please. It was dark, I couldn't see. . . .

BINGO:

(*to George*)
How about it, Georgie? Shall we teach her a lesson?

SALLY ANN:

Please, I made a mistake. I'm sorry.

BINGO:

You made a mistake all right. This (*She makes a sweeping gesture toward George.*) is George, a bonafide Royal Canadian Mounted Policeman, a real ballsy chap. And I'm his one and only Bingo, understand? A loyal flesh-and-blood Canadian girl who works in this human palace seven days a week. And you can't come in here off the street and insult George and me.

SALLY ANN:

(*looking down and trembling*)
I hate this place.

BINGO:
> She hates us, George.

SALLY ANN:
> Oh, I like you! You remind me of a girl I knew at home.

BINGO:
> Dream-girl of the provinces, that's me. You can ask George.

SALLY ANN:
> She was pretty.

BINGO:
> Well, but if you don't like the living statues—all thirty-eight true-to-life replicas of the most famous personages in the history of the old UK and a few less important countries of the world—what are you doing in here anyway? Just waiting for a friend?

SALLY ANN:
> Yes. Just waiting for a friend.

BINGO:
> Don't worry, he'll be along. But if he doesn't hurry it up we'll send George after him.
> (*to George*)
> OK, George?

SALLY ANN:
> He's here already.

BINGO:
> Here? Already? Maybe I was wrong about you after all. Let me guess.

(*She looks about the room in mock amazement.*)
Is it Prince Philip? Lord Nelson? The Duke of Windsor? I ought to warn you about Lord Nelson. He's got a hole in his chest as big as a teacup. He's not much good. But a girl couldn't go wrong on the old Duke of Windsor. No sir. But maybe it's Napoleon—is that it?
(*She laughs.*)
There's a fine little frisky chap for you, even if he is foreign. . . . Come on, come on, don't be afraid —I'm stuck with poor George here, you see—so let me in on the secret!

SALLY ANN:
(*looking down*)
I'm waiting for my boyfriend. He's downstairs—in the Chamber of Horrors. . . .

BINGO:
Oh. Your boyfriend.

SALLY ANN:
Yes.

BINGO:
Well, that's a bit of a letdown.
(*to George*)
Wouldn't you say so, George?
(*to Sally Ann*)
Sure you don't want me to fix you up with the Prince there or the Duke of Windsor? I'm on—familiar terms with all these chaps, you see.

SALLY ANN:
> My boyfriend wanted me to go down into the Chamber of Horrors with him, but I wouldn't. It's bad enough up here.

BINGO:
> Is it? Is it really so bad up here?

SALLY ANN:
> (*quickly*)
> If you're not used to it, I mean.

BINGO:
> Yes, I know what you mean. Well, don't worry. Your boyfriend will come back for you. There's a lucky streak in you—I can see that.

SALLY ANN:
> I know he will. And then we're going to be married.

BINGO:
> That's the ticket.

SALLY ANN:
> He's asked me already. I said I would.

BINGO:
> He popped the question and you—acquiesced. Is that it?

SALLY ANN:
> (*nodding*)
> I told him I would.

BINGO:
> Didn't think twice about it, did you.

> (*to George*)
> How's that for devotion, George?

SALLY ANN:
> He could have had any girl he wanted.
> (*nervously, gesturing toward George*)
> He—he looks like him.

(*Bingo whistles in mock amazement.*)

BINGO:
> (*to George*)
> How about that, George—a rival!

SALLY ANN:
> His name is Frank.

BINGO:
> And now he's gone off and left you.
> (*to George*)
> You men are all the same, my boy—no good!

SALLY ANN:
> I've got the fidgets.
> (*glancing over her shoulder*)
> I hate this place. It gives me shivers. Doesn't it give you shivers?

BINGO:
> You'd rather be out on the street with Frank, is that it?
> (*under her breath*)
> Well, who wouldn't!

SALLY ANN:
> We were walking along together eating ice cream.

The sun was warm, I could hardly see for the glare. A horse-drawn carriage was standing at the corner and I could smell the horse. And then Frank stops dead in his tracks and says, "Well, what do you know, Sally Ann, the wax museum! Let's have a look inside. You're only young once. You game?" I told him I wanted to go for a ride in the carriage like other people. But he said we could do that later. He said he just had to have a look at Cleopatra, Queen of the Nile.

BINGO:

*(laughing)*

They're all the same. They all want to see Cleopatra without her bra. Do you blame them?

SALLY ANN:

*(looking down)*

Not Frank. Frank's always been interested in history.

BINGO:

And Moose Neck Betty, Canada's own teenage call girl of the oil fields? Did he put Moose Neck Betty in historical perspective too?

SALLY ANN:

*(looking down)*

I—I wouldn't let him look at Moose Neck Betty.

BINGO:

*(laughing)*

He looked at her, all right—when your back was turned. And you know what he was thinking, don't you? They're all the same. George will tell you: Betty's got more in her navel than most people have in all their quivering guts heaped up in a pile. She's our only hope.

SALLY ANN:

She's been deported. She'll spend the rest of her life in the tropics, where she belongs.

BINGO:

(*to George*)
Tell the young lady, George—tell her Moose Neck Betty is right here, right here next to poor old Winnie, where she belongs! The young lady seems to have forgotten, George.

SALLY ANN:

(*glancing in the direction of the wax figures*)
I haven't forgotten. And—and I can't stand being in the same room with her. I hate her. I hate them all.

BINGO:

Say, what's the matter with you? She's just off the street like the rest of them. Like you and me. If you find Betty (*Pause*) repellent (*Pause*) you must be sick. She's every schoolgirl's heroine. She's our only hope.

SALLY ANN:

I just want Frank.

BINGO:

(*taking Sally Ann by the shoulders*)
Listen, Sal, I've been kidding. Frank doesn't have a dirty thought in his head about Moose Neck Betty,

he's not interested in Cleopatra. Because (*with emphasis, and shaking Sally Ann*) Frank is down in the Chamber of Horrors staring at Marie Antoinette with her head chopped off. He's a real ballsy chap, your Frank. Like my George here.

SALLY ANN:

(*in horror*)
With her head chopped off?

BINGO:

(*releasing her*)
That's right. Up here we've got the beauty, down there they've got the gore. People like a little bit of both in this world, Sal. Georgie knows.
(*to George*)
Don't you, George.
(*She raps his chest.*)

SALLY ANN:

(*staring at George*)
Frank said I needed a fright. . . .

BINGO:

(*brightly*)
He ought to know!

SALLY ANN:

He said there was no harm in it because they're only dummies anyway. . . .

BINGO:

(*under her breath*)
He'll find out!

SALLY ANN:

He said a little fright would do me good. He said it would be—fun!

BINGO:

That's a smart chap, your Frank. How can you be married if you haven't seen Marie Antoinette's head in a basket? You should have taken his word for it.

SALLY ANN:

(*wailing*)
But I'm frightened now . . . !

BINGO:

(*catching hold of her arm*)
Come off it, Sal. You haven't begun to live yet.

SALLY ANN:

(*wrenching free and whispering to George*)
Suppose Frank leaves me here? Suppose they take off all my clothes and stand me up beside—beside Moose Neck Betty for the rest of my life? What then?

BINGO:

(*laughing*)
Come off it, come off it, Sal. Quit dreaming.
(*to George*)
What do you think, George—a nice young girl with an education and an orchid on her, her bosom, George . . . . (*She winks.*) and going off to marry your rival Frank, and here she is worrying about spending the rest of her life in a wax museum. It's crazy, isn't it, George?

(*to Sally Ann, bitterly*)
You think you're me? You'd have something to worry about if you were me. I'm here for good.

SALLY ANN:

(*whispering to George*)
They'll turn me into a freak—won't they.

BINGO:

(*slowly*)
There are no freaks in this place, Sal. Just people.
(*She rises again to her happy irony.*)
But you're OK, Sal, you've got your man, he'll take you back outside—don't worry—and carry you off to a two-room flat where you can wash your underpants in the bathroom sink and drink 3.2 beer with the rest of the dead Canadians and wear Frank's ring like a set of little sharp teeth clamped to your finger and spill your cookies in the snow of old Montreal. You're the last of the virgins—but who wants to be a virgin?

SALLY ANN:

(*catching hold of George's shoulder*)
I'm sick. I've got to have some water.

BINGO:

There's a bubbler around the corner. Next to Tarzan. He's the only American in the house.

SALLY ANN:

I'm not going out there alone.

BINGO:

Frank will buy you a beer. Be patient. But nobody

will buy poor little Bingo a beer, I'm in this dump for life.
(*She smiles.*)
I'm George's bad girl. I'm his—prisoner of love.
(*She laughs, looks up at George.*)
Isn't that right, George?

SALLY ANN:
(*turning downstage*)
I have a sandwich in my bag. Maybe some food will help.

BINGO:
Sure, it'll settle your stomach. You virgins are all the same.
(*to George*)
That right, George?
(*to Sally Ann*)
I don't get anything but kisses in a little plastic bag from one day to the next. You ever tried living on chocolate kisses in a plastic bag?

(*Bingo drags the bench in front of George and she and Sally Ann sit down. Bingo eats, while holding George's hand.*)

SALLY ANN:
Have you—have you really seen Marie Antoinette?

BINGO:
(*eating*)
Sure I have. You could have seen her yourself.

SALLY ANN:
Is her head really—in a basket?

BINGO:
> Don't you believe me?

SALLY ANN:
> The poor thing. . . .

BINGO:
> She got what she wanted.
> (*She munches the sandwich.*)
> Her head's face-up in the basket. It's unnatural, but who wants to see the back of Marie Antoinette's head? It'd look just like the back of a Canadian's head. And Marie Antoinette was no Canadian, that's for sure.

SALLY ANN:
> (*unable to eat and giving her sandwich to Bingo*)
> You can really—see her face? How horrible.

BINGO:
> (*munching the sandwich*)
> It looks a little like the face of a virgin, come to think of it. Maybe she remembered herself as a virgin when the ax fell. Maybe under the blade she got pure again. Who knows? Say, that face down there looks a lot like yours.
> (*She grins up at George.*)
> How about that, George?

SALLY ANN:
> Please—I'm not as innocent as you think.

BINGO:
> (*laughing, munching the sandwich*)
> Come off it, Sal. I can tell at a glance. You may not

have any blood trickling out of your mouth, and your mouth might not be open as if you had swallowed an egg in its shell, and your eyes might not be painted the pale blue color of pain and happiness —but you've got a virgin's face if I ever saw one.

**SALLY ANN:**
Frank says it's good to be pure.

**BINGO:**
Frank, Frank .... what's Frank care about virginity? What would he be doing in the Chamber of Horrors if he cared about it? But Marie Antoinette is not the only suffering girl down there, believe me.
(*She eats.*)

**SALLY ANN:**
You mean—there are more atrocities down there?

**BINGO:**
(*pausing between bites.*)
Where did they bring you up, anyway? In one of our Canadian convents? Some old Canuck with a shaved head and rimless spectacles and rosy cheeks and long black robes and deflated breasts—deflated, you know—drew the veil in front of your eyes forever, did she? Is that it?
(*She eats.*)

**SALLY ANN:**
(*swaying on the bench and slowly removing her hat*)
I've had a normal life.

**BINGO:**

>(*laughing*)
>Normal? Normal?
>(*to George*)
>You hear that, George?
>(*to Sally Ann*)
>A girl who's never been in the Chamber of Horrors—that's normal? You think that's normal?
>(*She shakes her head.*)
>They've kept you in brutal ignorance, my girl. Brutal ignorance.
>(*She eats.*)

(*Sally Ann gropes for George's other hand, but cannot find it.*)

**SALLY ANN:**

>(*trying to summon her courage*)
>I know some of the facts of life, I tell you.

**BINGO:**

>The facts of life? You?
>(*She laughs.*)
>You're ignorant, that's what you are. You're blind all over. They haven't broken your seal yet. They never will.

**SALLY ANN:**

>(*looking about wildly, calling in a small voice for help*)
>Frank . . . ? Where are you, Frank . . . ?

(*Pause. Then Bingo leans forward and gives Sally Ann a gentle push.*)

BINGO:
> (*kindly, humorously*)
> He's down there all right, don't worry. Just down there ogling Joan of Arc among the clergy.

SALLY ANN:
> Saint Joan?

BINGO:
> (*nodding*)
> Would you believe it? Joan of Arc with her armor all ripped off. It's quite a sight.

SALLY ANN:
> (*giggling, trying to convince herself*)
> Oh, you're teasing me. I should have known. You're just teasing me....

BINGO:
> (*still kindly*)
> You can't blame them. They were only trying to prove she was a woman. Like you. Like me. They couln't leave off even when she was in the fire. Ask Frank, ask Georgie here. They're all the same.
> (*She licks her fingers, wipes them fastidiously on her tunic, glances at Sally Ann, who tries to loosen her collar.*)
> She was ignorant, but she had pretty legs, that Joan of Arc.
> (*casually*)
> Not as pretty as your legs, though.

SALLY ANN:
> (*looking down*)
> There's nothing pretty about me.

BINGO:
> Come off it, Sal.
> (*She laughs.*)
> Hasn't Frank ever told you you've got attractive legs?

SALLY ANN:
> (*primly, sadly*)
> Frank has never noticed my legs. He's not that kind.

BINGO:
> A celibate! A real celibate!
> (*She rises, walks around the bench and leans on George.*)
> That's one thing you can say for George—he's not reticent. He's not a celibate.

SALLY ANN:
> Frank is a very silent man.

BINGO:
> Think so? You wait and see.

SALLY ANN:
> Frank wouldn't talk about my legs. I—I wouldn't want him to.

BINGO:
> (*to George*)
> What are we going to do with her, my boy? She's hopeless.
> (*She removes George's hat and fixes it with military severity on her own head.*)
> A real problem, this bride-to-be.

## THE WAX MUSEUM

SALLY ANN:

Frank says I have a good disposition.

BINGO:

Mary, queen of all the stupid girls in Canada—you hear that?
(*She walks around the bench again, sits down.*)
Down there with his heart going a hundred miles an hour and his eyes popping out of his head at the sight of an aborted baby being carried off by a cat —garden variety tomcat, Sally Ann—and a thirteen-year-old girl heretic stretched out naked on the rack and the Lord High Executioner and a whole bunch of ballsy chaps shoving a white hot poker up King Richard's skinny old rump . . . .
(*Sally Ann begins to writhe on the bench.*)
and Jack-the-Ripper cutting up a fish girl in Haymarket Square and a ninety-year-old Chinaman burning incense and gouging out the eyes of a coolie on his knees and a big black African prince with zebra stripes drinking the blood of a missionary's beautiful young wife and Frank, your Frank, talking about a good disposition!
(*She pushes the hat onto the back of her head, opens the top button of her tunic.*)

SALLY ANN:

(*smiling tensely at Bingo as in a trance*)
I see that poor little baby in the jaws of the cat. I see it.

BINGO:

The whole world is hungry, Sally Ann.

SALLY ANN:
>I smell the blood....

BINGO:
>Blood and ecstasy, that's the ticket.

SALLY ANN:
>And I see the fish girl in Haymarket Square.

BINGO:
>She stinks, you can bet your life. But that Jack-the-Ripper's a wild one, there's no stopping him.

SALLY ANN:
>And there's the missionary's wife with her forgiving eyes.

BINGO:
>(*laughing*)
>You're hopeless—a real bride-to-be!

SALLY ANN:
>And the little girl on the rack—how small she is, how white. What small ribs she has like—like fingers around her chest!

BINGO:
>Don't forget Bluebeard. There's a lovely one of Bluebeard with his youngest wife.
>(*She laughs.*)
>That's what you're going to be, Sal. The youngest wife.

SALLY ANN:
>(*desperately catching hold of Bingo's arm*)
>But Frank's down there!

(*looking around her*)
Frank's alone down there!

BINGO:
(*softly*)
He's not alone.

SALLY ANN:
He's alone down there smelling the blood.

BINGO:
Frank is having a good time. He's enjoying himself.

SALLY ANN:
Alone down there staring at the head of Marie Antoinette. Alone and wanting to kiss the lips of her poor severed head.

BINGO:
(*to herself*)
Why doesn't it rot? Why doesn't her head rot?

SALLY ANN:
I should have obeyed him. I should have gone into the Chamber of Horrors and held Frank's hand!

BINGO:
Don't worry, he'll be back. He can't spend all day down there. He'll come back to you a different man, don't worry.
(*She laughs.*)

SALLY ANN:
I suppose he will.

BINGO:
> He'll come back ravenous, you'll see. He'll come rushing up to the lavatory and buy his packet of "Pro-Long"—you know about "Pro-Long," don't you, Sally Ann? Well, think about it, figure it out for yourself, just concentrate—and he'll rush in here with his hair all slicked down and grab you and carry you off to a bloody honeymoon in that two-room flat. You'll see. Frank's no celibate. Not Frank.

SALLY ANN:
> I'm frightened.
> (*whispering*)
> I'm frightened, Bingo. I'm not—not Cleopatra, Bingo. I'm just poor Sally Ann, and I'm frightened.

BINGO:
> (*kindly but urgently*)
> If I had your legs and your (*relenting a little*) disposition, I wouldn't be frightened—not me—I wouldn't care if I did have to live my life in a wax museum.
> (*She puts her hand on Sally Ann's thigh.*)
> Your legs are beautiful. Your orchid's beautiful. You've got a pretty face. Didn't Frank ever tell you? Your legs are prettier than mine, prettier than Joan of Arc's.
> (*She pushes Sally Ann's skirt as high as she can.*)
> Don't you see? How white they are, and long and thin.

(*Unconsciously but intensely, she runs her hand up and down Sally Ann's leg.*)
It's just like George told me: "You've got legs like Moose Neck Betty's, Bingo, honest to God. There's no hair on her legs, Bingo, and there's none on yours." That's what he said, honest to God. Only he was talking about you, Sally Ann, not me! And he was right. And look, you've even got silk stockings on. Silk stockings!
(*She inspects the stockings.*)
If I had stockings like those I'd walk out of this palace free as air, I'd walk right out with George. We'd pack our little traveling bags and jump on the first bus and go all the way to Niagara Falls. We'd arrive in the middle of the afternoon in the height of the season—can't you see it, Sally Ann?—and we'd leave our bags in the depot and rush to the Falls. And then I'd let old George take me right on the banks of Niagara Falls. Can't you see it? Indecent behavior in a public place! We'd throw our clothes over the falls, me in just my stockings and George in his boots, and then we'd hold hands and stand there while the tourists got out their home movie cameras and fired away!

SALLY ANN:
(*passionately*)
Take them....

BINGO:
What?

**SALLY ANN:**

Take the stockings. They're yours.
(*She smiles.*)

**BINGO:**

(*kneeling and removing the stockings*)
That's the ticket! I knew you'd say that, Sal. You're better off with your legs bare, aren't you, Sal? You want to show off your white skin, Sally Ann. Have you ever looked at your foot? Ten little fat toes for a lucky man, eh, Sal? Oh, there's no hair on your legs, Sally Ann. No hair at all. Just skin that wants to crawl when you touch it.
(*She draws on the stockings hastily.*)

**SALLY ANN:**

Do they—do they fit?

**BINGO:**

Yes, they fit. They're as smooth as wax. . . .
(*displaying her leg*)
they're gorgeous!

**SALLY ANN:**

(*displaying her leg, wiggling and arching her foot*)
I've never seen my foot before.
(*She laughs.*)

**BINGO:**

George is crazy about bare feet.

**SALLY ANN:**

In the swimming pool in the Young Girls' Club back home I caught the itch. A terrible itch between the toes.

BINGO:

> (*to George*)
> What are we going to do with her, George? She's morbid!

SALLY ANN:

> I took the home cure—it was successful. I've got clean feet now.

BINGO:

> You're hopeless.

SALLY ANN:

> (*displaying her leg*)
> Am I really better off with—bare legs?

BINGO:

> George is crazy about bare legs. He's got his eye on you, my girl.

SALLY ANN:

> I've always been just a thin girl with stringy hair, packed in a community swimming pool with other thin girls with stringy hair. My life has always been —disinfected. I'm not—glamorous. The only man who ever looked at me was the owner of a drive-in restaurant. He was bald and had a carving knife stuck in his apron. His eyes were like beef soup. I felt so—debased.

BINGO:

> You missed your chance. You might have thought he was a horny Canuck, but he was really Blackie-the-Butcher. You missed your chance!

SALLY ANN:
> Frank's different. George is different too.

BINGO:
> George doesn't need any "Pro-Long," that's for sure!
> (*She laughs.*)

SALLY ANN:
> I think I could trust myself with George.

BINGO:
> He's a Mounty, old George is. He means business. There's no stopping George.
> (*She gives his hand a squeeze.*)

SALLY ANN:
> He has a nice red coat.

BINGO:
> That's the ticket. He's got a red coat.

SALLY ANN:
> And a nice smile.

BINGO:
> Happy-go-lucky chap, that's George.

SALLY ANN:
> He wouldn't make me cry.

BINGO:
> (*to George*)
> How about that, George? Would you make her cry?

SALLY ANN:

>But if he did I wouldn't care. He's so big, he's so respectable....

BINGO:

>(*to George*)
>How about that, George—respectable!

SALLY ANN:

>And I'm attractive. I'm good enough for George. Didn't you say I'm beautiful and glamorous and pure? Let them put me on the rack, I don't care. Let the black man drink my blood, I don't care. George will look after me, I've got soft skin and a good disposition.... What are you doing?

(*Bingo unbuttons her red tunic, leans toward Sally Ann. Bingo's red brassiere is visible.*)

>Why are you doing that?
>(*She pauses in alarm, then leans away from Bingo seductively, thrusts out one leg.*)
>Frank will be sorry he didn't take me to the Chamber of Horrors. He'll be sorry he left me up here all alone. He'll find out he can't abandon me this way, he'll find out something about the power of my virginity. He'll see.... What are you doing?

(*Bingo unbuttons the jacket of Sally Ann's traveling suit. Sally Ann is also wearing a red brassiere, now visible.*)

Please, please, why are you doing that? You've got my stockings, aren't they enough? What more do you want?

(*Bingo slips the jacket off one shoulder, caresses her.*)

Oh, do something, George, save me. . . .

BINGO:

It's the witching hour in the wax museum, Sally Ann. It's time for love.

SALLY ANN:

(*as Bingo caresses her*)
Please, please. . . . What's happening? What are you doing to me? Dear God—why didn't you take me to the bubbler and let me drink? Why didn't you let me wait outside? Oh George, George—don't touch me. Please. I'm young and pure and plain, I've taken the home cure, George. . . .

BINGO:

(*her face close to Sally Ann's*)
You're beautiful, you're our only hope.

SALLY ANN:

I could never swim anything but the sidestroke in the community pool. I always swallowed water. Once they took me to Saskatchewan and I vomited in the car—don't you understand me? Don't you hear what I'm saying? I've always had a terrible emptiness inside my head, I never knew how to fix my hair, even now I sit with my knees together. . . . What are you doing?

(*She struggles.*)
Oh my God, what next?

(*Bingo removes Sally Ann's jacket, kisses her neck and shoulders, caresses her.*)

> George, dear George. . . . What next? Oh can't you see that I'm unwilling?
> (*Her sensual struggles belie her words.*)
> Can't you see I'm afraid of the little baby in the cat's jaws? Can't you see I'm afraid? Oh, why can't you just leave me to my soap and water and bobby pins and lonely walks in the sunshine? Why can't you leave me alone? I always had to walk home from school alone. Please, please, I'm just like Queen Elizabeth. . . !

(*Bingo kisses her long and brutally.*)

BINGO:
> (*drawing away from her slowly*)
> Now be quiet. She's the same as everyone else.

SALLY ANN:
> (*whispering*)
> What have you done?

BINGO:
> You were born for this place, you're worth the price of anyone's admission. You're beautiful, you'll live forever, like the rest of them. You know what they'll write on your little cardboard sign for the tourists? "Young Canadian Woman in the Throes of Love"!

**SALLY ANN:**

It's not true! Please. . . . I'm not that kind of girl. I want to go riding in a horse-drawn carriage with the man I married. I just want to sit there with my hands in my lap and the orchid fluttering on my chest. I. . . .

**BINGO:**

Love is for you and me and George—dirty old George—and Frank. Didn't anyone tell you that before?
(*She caresses her again with deep affection.*)
It's fun. Isn't it?
(*Slowly she puts George's wide-brimmed hat on the back of Sally Ann's head.*)

**SALLY ANN:**

(*looking into Bingo's eyes, then looking down, becoming confused and beginning to laugh.*)
Yes. Oh yes. Everybody knows it's fun but me.
(*She laughs warmly.*)
Even poor old Lord Nelson!

**BINGO:**

(*laughing, caressing her*)
You can see it in the old boy's eye.

**SALLY ANN:**

(*excitedly, with self-insight*)
I don't want to ride in a carriage—how did I get that idea?
(*She laughs.*)

BINGO:

It's just one of the attractions of romantic Canada, that's all.

SALLY ANN:

You know what I want? I've known it all along.
(*She looks happily into Bingo's eyes.*)
I've always wanted a big man in a bright red coat to take me within full view of kings and queens and school children in a wax museum—at noon!

BINGO:

"Young Canadian Woman in the Throes of Love"!

SALLY ANN:

But that uniform—that off that awful uniform!
(*She leans forward tentatively, then embraces Bingo happily.*)

BINGO:

Old George is an obliging chap. You'll see. Naked flanks and a good heart—that's George. Quick now, he's waiting. . . .

(*They laugh. Bingo removes her tunic and helps Sally Ann to put it on. Then Bingo puts on Sally Ann's jacket, picks up the pocketbook. They stand. Sally Ann faces George while Bingo walks around the bench, takes George by the arm and speaks to him with affection.*)

And so, George, another conquest. Take care of her, my boy. She has pretty legs. Poor George—the little boys yank your coat-tails and put candy wrappers in your pockets and punch you below the

belt, and the young girls swoon and swipe your hat and ruffle your hair. That's what comes of having a good heart, George. Even the old mothers love you, my boy. And they don't know the half of it.
(*She laughs and strokes his hair.*)
I won't forget. But now it's good-by, George. The time has come. . . .

FRANK:

(*bellowing offstage*)
Sally Ann—for Christ's sake quit hiding, Sally Ann, it's time to go. Don't keep me waiting, baby, for Christ's sake!

BINGO:

(*embracing George, then moving toward upstage exit*)
That's me, my boy. It's time to go. Good-by, George.
(*to Sally Ann*)
Remember now, don't touch the wax. It's poison.

(*She exits. Lights start down slowly. Sally Ann comes out of her trance and approaches George radiantly, begins to fondle him.*)

SALLY ANN:

Just look at you. Pocket open (*She buttons it*), collar undone (*She fastens it.*), going around without your hat (*She takes it off and puts it on his head.*)—you're a mess, George. A regular disgrace. You need a woman, my boy. That's what you need.

(*Lights fade almost to darkness. Sally Ann caresses George and rubs herself against him with violent sensuality.*)

That's the ticket, George. A good woman. Somebody you can hold in your arms and fill with joy, somebody who doesn't mind a little blood on the floor. . . .

(*Stage goes to full darkness while she continues to speak.*)

That me, George, I'm your girl. (*moaning*) Georgie? Georgie? Take care of me, George. . . .

## CURTAIN

# THE UNDERTAKER

*An old-fashioned lavatory represented on a bare stage by a wooden platform with four downstage steps and containing a large white glistening porcelain tub with heavy claws, a highly polished white toilet with brightly varnished blond wooden seat and lid, and a large marble sink. A pull chain hangs from the darkness overhead, and suspended above the sink and toilet are a marble shelf containing a large black shaving mug with brush and a large rectangle of opaque green glass, representing a window. There is a large Victorian pitcher on a small white table, and to the right of the toilet a white hat rack bearing a long-unused woman's negligee and enormous white garden hat. The pitcher contains several long-stemmed waxen lilies haphazardly arranged.*

FATHER. *A small-town undertaker in his mid-forties. He wears a black suit with a flower in his lapel and a stickpin in his somber tie.*

EDWARD. *The undertaker's son, also in his mid-forties. He wears a contemporary light-colored business suit with a white handkerchief protruding from the breast pocket, and a lurid tie.*

*Lights up dimly to reveal father seated bolt upright on the toilet lid and holding an old-fashioned silver revolver at right angles to his temple. His face is bright with perspiration and he stares directly and brilliantly at the audience. Suddenly, he is caught in a burst of light suggesting the phosphorescent explosion of a photographer's flash powder, and for a moment smiles. The stage goes dark immediately and from offstage in the darkness come the awkward sounds of a child practicing a cello. The sounds start and stop, a phrase or two is repeated, the music trails into silence. Lights up on the empty lavatory.*

EDWARD:

*(offstage)*
Papa, wait, Papa, please. . . .

FATHER:

*(offstage)*
Stop it, Edward. Leave me alone.

EDWARD:

*(offstage)*
Don't, Papa. Wait for me.

FATHER:

*(offstage)*
Hands off, Edward. Do as I say.

*(sounds of scuffling)*

EDWARD:

*(offstage)*
Papa, Papa, please. . . .

(*Father enters at a clumsy fast stride from stage right and clutching a small oblong cardboard box. He pauses midstage, wheels, rushes once around the lavatory, again pauses midstage, stares about him in distraction, backs away with as much dignity as possible as Edward enters from stage right at a helpless half-run.*)

EDWARD:
> You threw me down!

FATHER:
> Stop it, Edward. Keep away.

EDWARD:
> You knocked me down, Papa. You pushed me.

FATHER:
> Keep off, Edward. Keep your distance.

EDWARD:
> How could you do it, Papa?

FATHER:
> (*pausing, breathing heavily*)
> Are you out of your mind? I've never laid a hand on you, Edward. Not once.

EDWARD:
> What about Mama? What would she think?

FATHER:
> (*startled, on guard again*)
> Keep away from me, Edward. Hands off!

EDWARD:
> I won't hurt you, Papa.

## THE UNDERTAKER

**FATHER:**

Stop it! Keep your hands to yourself.

**EDWARD:**

(*inching forward*)
It's your work, Papa. It makes you morbid.

**FATHER:**

Damn it, Edward, what do you know about my work?

**EDWARD:**

I've tried to please you, Papa. I've done my best.

**FATHER:**

Wasted effort. Wasted effort. All of it. But I'll tell you something, Edward. I've been father and mother both to you. Remember that. I'm as good as your own mother was any day. Remember that.

**EDWARD:**

I love you, Papa. . . .

**FATHER:**

(*backing abruptly to stage left corner of lavatory*)
Stop it!

**EDWARD:**

Just let me hold your hand, Papa. Please. . . .

**FATHER:**

Don't take another step.
(*He breathes heavily, glances sternly about the stage, grows more calm and fondles the box absently.*)
Don't move.

(*He looks at the box then stares at Edward, takes a breath.*)
My work has nothing to do with it. Not a thing. For twenty years—twenty years, Edward—I've embalmed the corpses of penniless Negroes and financed their purchases of suitable caskets at reasonable rates out of my own pocket. And I enjoyed every minute of it, Edward.

EDWARD:

You can't frighten me, Papa. I'm not afraid of dead people.

FATHER:

I'm not trying to frighten you, damn it. Can't you be reasonable, just for once? There's nothing wrong with dead Negroes. Nothing at all.

EDWARD:

But Mama's dead too. That's wrong, isn't it?

FATHER:

You're impossible.

EDWARD:

I know she's dead. You told me yourself.

FATHER:

But I'm your mother now. I've been your mother for years. Remember that.

EDWARD:

I will, Papa. I will.

**FATHER:**
> But you're afraid of the dead Negroes, aren't you, Edward? You're scared to death of them.
> (*He chuckles, grows stern again.*)
> Why don't you admit it for once in your life?

**EDWARD:**
> You protect me.... you take good care of me....

**FATHER:**
> That's enough...!

**EDWARD:**
> And I love you, Papa.

**FATHER:**
> Stop...!

**EDWARD:**
> I just want to sit on your lap, Papa, I want to feel your beard.

**FATHER:**
> Damnation!
> (*He wheels and rushes around the lavatory, appears stage right and backs slowly and suspiciously to a halt.*)
> Damnation!

(*Edward faces his father and wrings his hands.*)

> I'm going to carry out this business in my own house. Damned if I'm not. And if they rise up out of the cold ground like a mob of raving minstrels and try to stop me, I'll fight them off. Every last one of them. There's gratitude for you....

**EDWARD:**
> Papa, Papa, don't forget me, please. . . . I want to be with you, Papa, I want to help. . . .

**FATHER:**
> (*after a moment of shocked silence*)
> You? You? I've had enough of you. I will not tolerate you any longer.
> (*He raises the box to his ear and shakes it.*)
> I will not tolerate this interference any longer.

**EDWARD:**
> What's the matter, Papa? What have I done?

**FATHER:**
> (*laughing, then pulling himself up abruptly*)
> There you go again. Worry, worry, worry. Why must you worry all the time?
> (*He pulls a handkerchief from his hip pocket and wipes his face.*)
> There's nothing the matter. You've done nothing. You're innocent. You're just the innocent son of a middle-aged small-town undertaker.
> (*He stuffs the handkerchief into his coat pocket.*)
> But I've planted the seeds of death in you, Edward. At least I've done that much anyway.

**EDWARD:**
> Have you, Papa?

**FATHER:**
> Yes, I have, damn it. The seeds of death.

**EDWARD:**
> Poor Papa, you're trembling. . . .

FATHER:
> I'm as cool as springwater. I've got a mind of ice. So don't worry about me, Edward. Just look to your own troubles. Just give a little thought to all those dead Negroes coming after you in the night.

EDWARD:
> Mama told me never to be afraid.

FATHER:
> She did, did she?

EDWARD:
> Yes, Papa, that's what she said.

FATHER:
> (*pausing deliberately, holding the box to his ear*) Edward, how old are you?

EDWARD:
> I'm twelve years old, Papa. I was twelve last May. Don't you remember? Don't you remember my big layer cake with white frosting and pink flowers? You said it looked like a sarcophagus and sang happy birthday to me while I lit the candles, and . . . .

FATHER:
> Then why the devil aren't you in school, Edward? Go to school, for God's sake, and leave me alone.

EDWARD:
> It's summer, Papa. It's July.

FATHER:
> Go to school anyway, for God's sake. What's the difference? The janitor will let you in. The best

concentration is in an empty schoolhouse—any fool knows that. Don't let the summer vacation stop you, Edward. Go sit in that empty schoolhouse and improve your mind while the rest of the fools are off nagging their parents at little stagnant lake resorts around the nation. Go think about the Negroes and the seeds of death.... Go do something, Edward—anything—your father's tired now. He's busy.
(*He wipes his face.*)

EDWARD:
I want to whisper something in your ear.

FATHER:
No!

EDWARD:
(*inching forward*)
It's urgent, Papa. Just this once.

FATHER:
By God, Edward....

EDWARD:
I'm desperate, Papa. Don't deny me.
(*He approaches his father as he would a shy horse.*)
Let me whisper in your ear. Just once. I'll die if you don't.

FATHER:
You're making it difficult for me, Edward. You're trying my patience.

**EDWARD:**

> (*approaching closer*)
> Just a few soft whispered words, Papa. Please....

**FATHER:**

> Be quick about it, Edward. There isn't much time.

(*Edward speaks awkwardly into his father's ear. Father sighs, puts his hand on Edward's shoulder, then turns downstage abruptly.*)

> Now? Now? You want to go walking in the garden with your mother at a time like this? Impossible...!

**EDWARD:**

> Now, Papa! Right this minute! For the sake of your son, Papa.

**FATHER:**

> I might have known you'd think of some such nonsense, Edward. You're a persistent child.

**EDWARD:**

> But you'll do it, won't you? Just for me?

**FATHER:**

> The devil take it, Edward—be quick now.

(*From offstage come the labored sounds of the child practicing his cello as Edward embraces his father, turns, climbs the lavatory steps and returns with the woman's hat and negligee, which Father puts on. The cello continues to play while, hand in hand, the two walk up and down as in a garden.*)

EDWARD:
> Shall I get the trowel?

FATHER:
> Never mind the trowel. We won't need it now.

EDWARD:
> You forgot your fan. Shall I get your fan? It's warm.

FATHER:
> You're right, Edward. It is warm. It's always warm in July. But never mind the fan.
> (*pausing, as if to study the leaves on a low branch*)
> My fan wouldn't help the poor leaves, Edward. The leaves are thirsty.

EDWARD:
> The worms are thirsty too, Mama. I'll attach the hose.

FATHER:
> (*smiling*)
> God will send water for the leaves and flowers and worms when the sun goes down, Edward. You'll see.

(*They continue to walk.*)

EDWARD:
> But don't you even want to prune the roses, Mama?

FATHER:
> (*smiling, shaking his head*)
> Go thou thy way, and I go mine;
>   Apart, yet not afar,
> Only a thin veil hangs between
>   The pathways where we are. . . .

EDWARD:

(*stopping*)
Mama? I want to tell you my dream. May I tell it, Mama?

FATHER:

Yes, Edward. Tell me the dream.

EDWARD:

Well, it's always the same. I see you in the doorway of a big white house on a hill. There are clouds piled up behind the house and the morning sun is buried inside the clouds. There is no one else in that house, which is covered with white chimneys and shuttered windows. Well, you step down from under the portico, Mama, and raise a gentle hand to your hat. Then you lift your face and turn it left and right as if you're a royal lady trying to greet some prince or maybe an executioner with your lovely smile. Then you are moving, your skin and veins and hat and face all reflecting the peach and rose color of the sun. You descend one lichen-covered step and then another, sway and climb up beside the driver of a small open yellow auto with wooden wheels, white solid tires and brass head-lamps. The auto is thumping up and down, Mama, but silently. Behind the single high seat is strapped a little white satin trunk—your trunk, Mama. And the driver, I see, wears a white driving cap and white driving coat, great eyeless goggles and a black muffler wrapped about his throat and hiding his mouth and nose and chin. With one gloved hand he grips a lever as tall and thin as a sword, and there is a sudden flashing when he contracts his arm. With his other hand he is squeezing the black bulb of the horn—though I hear nothing—and is sitting even straighter against the wind. And now he is gripping the steering wheel, holding it at arm's length, and now he turns his head and takes a single long look into your face, Mama, and I see that you are admiring him—or pitying him—and I quiver. And then, Mama, the tires are rolling, the trunk swaying, the muffler beating the air, and suddenly the white coat is brown with the dust of the road and the little auto, severe and shiny like a golden insect, is gaining speed, and I see that you are serene, Mama, serene and unshaken as the downward ride commences, and are merely touching your fingers to the crown of your hat and raising a soft white arm as if to wave to me, and . . . .

FATHER:

(*pulling away*)
Edward! Stop it, Edward!
(*He throws down the hat, struggles out of the negligee and drops it. Sounds of the cello fade.*)
Is this your idea of a joke? Are you trying to trick me, Edward, and desecrate the memory of your mother?

EDWARD:

No, Papa, no. . . .

**FATHER:**
> Well, I'm not going to have it, do you understand?

**EDWARD:**
> Let me finish, Papa....

**FATHER:**
> Your mother never pitied me in her life!

**EDWARD:**
> Please, Papa....

**FATHER:**
> And I'll tell you, something, Edward. She died in bed, with blood all over the sheets. Blood. Do you hear?

**EDWARD:**
> Don't, Papa, please....

**FATHER:**
> But I'll destroy this nonsense once and for all. Damned if I won't.
> (*He runs to the lavatory steps and climbs them.*)

**EDWARD:**
> You were driving the car, Papa, you took her away. And now you're trying to kill me too!

**FATHER:**
> (*turning*)
> I'm trying to kill myself, Edward. It has nothing to to do with you. Nothing at all.
> (*He smiles and raises the box to his ear.*)

(*Sounds of the cello commence as the lights grow dim, revealing merely the silhouette of Father, who sits on the toilet lid and removes the revolver from the box on his knees and holds it at right angles to his temple. The phosphorescent light flashes, as in the beginning, and for a moment the stage goes to full dark. Sounds of the cello cease abruptly. Lights up slowly on Father, who sits with the still unopened box on his knees, and who is now visible to the audience but not to Edward, and on Edward who is now crouching on the lavatory steps.*)

EDWARD:
>You didn't mean it, Papa. Tell me you didn't.

FATHER:
>(*startled, seizing the box in both hands, then recalling himself and speaking as through a closed door*)
>I shall do it, Edward. See if I don't.

EDWARD:
>But why? Why?

FATHER:
>Some things, Edward, can't be helped.
>(*He loosens his tie, opens his collar and coat, wipes his face with the handkerchief which he stuffs again into his coat pocket.*)
>Are you there, Edward? I warn you, don't try to go for assistance.
>(*He listens.*)
>I'm as good as dead already. If you hadn't interfered, Edward, both of us would have been spared

the pain of this little discussion. But you're a stubborn child. You know that, don't you?

EDWARD:
> (*pausing*)
> Yes, Papa.

FATHER:
> Good. I'm glad we understand each other.
> (*He slips up the lid of the box, peers inside.*)
> Another thing, Edward. You weigh too much. A boy of—twelve—shouldn't weigh as much as you do.

EDWARD:
> (*pausing*)
> That's right, Papa. I'm big for my age.

FATHER:
> (*removing the lid of the box entirely and squinting, holding the box to the light*)
> You're fat, Edward. You've got too much stomach. You're too big in the arms and thighs. It's unhealthy.

EDWARD:
> Yes, Papa.

FATHER:
> In my twenty years as an undertaker, most of the Negroes I embalmed were either all fat or all bones. You must try to be somewhere in between, Edward.
> (*Pause*)
> Are you there?

(*He looks at the door.*)
Answer me, Edward.

**EDWARD:**
I'm here, Papa.

**FATHER:**
Good.
(*He again turns his attention to the box, on impulse takes a long sniff of it.*)
Most of my Negroes were preachers. You didn't know that, did you. Preachers or the relatives of preachers. Big fat black men of God or little black shriveled sacks with the calling still in their little protruding bones. The poor devils.
(*He listens suspiciously.*)
I was going to be a preacher myself, once. What do you think of that, Edward?
(*He leans forward, watches the door.*)

**EDWARD:**
(*pausing*)
That's very interesting, Papa.

**FATHER:**
I'm glad you think so.
(*He stares into the box.*)
Edward, I'll tell you something—the revolver is silver. You might as well know that much, anyway.

**EDWARD:**
Put it away, put it away, Papa.

**FATHER:**
> (*smiling*)
> I haven't taken it out of the box yet, Edward. Have patience, your father will blow his brains out in a moment. You can't stop me, Edward, even those damn raving minstrels—preachers, all of them—can't stop me.

**EDWARD:**
> (*whispering*)
> Papa, Papa, Papa. . . .

**FATHER:**
> What did you say, Edward?
> (*He listens.*)
> It's not as brutal as you think, my boy. It's just like jumping off a tandem bicycle into a little silvery pool on a hot day in July. Nothing to it. And somebody's always left, Edward. That's what counts.

**EDWARD:**
> (*pausing*)
> Papa?

(*Father stands up abruptly, watches the door.*)
> Come out of the lavatory. Please.

**FATHER:**
> (*laughing briefly*)
> You'd like that, wouldn't you. You'd like me to unlock the door and come out, towel and shaving mug in hand, and tell you the whole thing was a bad dream and that the old black fellow didn't have

his claws around my heart after all, and that I'll always be here to embalm the Negroes and listen to your prayers at night. Isn't that so, Edward?
(*He scowls, then smiles.*)
Well, it won't do. You can't trick me, Edward. I've still got a head on my shoulders, thank God for that. The Negroes will have to find somebody else. So will you.
(*He places the box on the toilet lid, moves to the sink, picks up the shaving mug and brush, turns on the tap, then speaks over his shoulder.*)
It's no dream, Edward. It's merely the simple act of a cold mind. I'm going to jump off the tandem bicycle, that's all.
(*He raises the mug and brush and inspects them.*)

EDWARD:

(*listening to the running water*)
Papa? Are you shaving?

FATHER:

(*turning off the water, replacing the mug and brush*)
No, Edward. I have shaved already today, thank you.

EDWARD:

(*pausing*)
I want to smell the toilet water on your cheek, Papa.

FATHER:

(*smiling and seizing the lilies, pulling them from the pitcher and holding them up, inspecting them*)

You've tried that tack already, Edward. It won't do. But sit on my lap, hold my hand, feel my beard, smell the toilet water—you're so physical, Edward. It's the disappointment of my life. I hate to see you depending on such—rubbish. Because that's what it is, all these ear lobes and tender veins and wrinkles that appear in a waxen brow and toenails and cloth and a bit of filling in a tooth—just so much rubbish. After all, I've spent my own life disposing of the remains. I ought to know.
(*He tosses the lilies into the bathtub and smiles.*)

EDWARD:

(*pausing*)
Papa? Is the water warm enough?

FATHER:

(*startled*)
I've turned it off already. I'm not shaving now. I told you that.
(*He peers at the sink, reaches out his hand slowly and tightens the tap.*)

EDWARD:

But it's dripping, Papa.

FATHER:

Nonsense. The tap is not dripping.
(*He leans down slowly and listens.*)

EDWARD:

I hear it, Papa. Don't you? There's a little singing noise in the sink. It must be leaking, Papa.

**FATHER:**

*(kneeling, inspecting the pipe beneath the sink, then standing, brushing off his knees, seizing the box and facing the door)*

Your little ruses don't fool me, Edward. There's nothing in here but the sound of the breath in my own nose. It's like the sound of butter being spread on toast—one more disturbance, Edward, one more fly on the pile of rubbish. But there's no water in the tap and soon there will be no breath in my nose. We'll turn it off tight—won't we, Edward?—like the tap.

*(He gives the tap a final peremptory twist, again faces the door.)*

But why can't I embalm myself? Why? There might be a certain pleasure if I could embalm myself. To part your own hair in the middle for the last time, to jerk the fancy tie into place around your own throat, to turn your own body into a rubber effigy and to take care of the eyelids with your own hands—at least there would be a certain satisfaction in disposing of your own rubbish, Edward, don't you agree?

*(He listens.)*

Well, what about it, Edward?

**EDWARD:**

*(pausing)*

You can't do all that to yourself. You can't.

**FATHER:**

That's right, Edward. It's impossible. A pathetic impossibility.

*(He sits on the lid of the toilet and partially removes the lid of the box, peers inside.)*

**EDWARD:**

But you could have been a preacher, Papa. I wish you had been a preacher.

**FATHER:**

*(smiling)*
Ah yes, I might well have been one of the raving minstrels. I might have been an excellent matchmaker between Christ and the old ladies. But I prefer my way, Edward. I prefer the rubbish reduced to rubbish.
*(He pauses, then raises the box and gives it several vigorous shakes.)*
Do you hear that, Edward? Revolver and bullets. Revolver and bullets, Edward. An old-fashioned toy for a man of strict principles.
*(He laughs.)*

**EDWARD:**

Let me see them, Papa. Let me have the box. . . .

**FATHER:**

*(wagging a finger at the door)*
No you don't, Edward. No you don't. The revolver and bullets are mine, my boy. You'll never see them. For the sake of discretion and selfishness, if you like, you'll never see them. You must accept impossibility also, Edward. You must grow as thin as I am and as clearheaded.
*(Slowly he removes the revolver from the box and dangles it before his face.)*

I begged your mother not to die. But there was no stopping your mother. She was a princess.
(*He studies the revolver.*)
And there's no stopping me, I can tell you that. You'll be lucky if you even catch a glimpse of my naked foot inside my black shoe, Edward. You'll never be an undertaker. I prefer that you see nothing when they carry me out of here.

EDWARD:

I won't move, I won't let you go. I'll crouch here forever if I have to, Papa. You'll see.

FATHER:

(*smiling*)
Distance is everywhere, Edward. This is the only way to make it real. And I'll tell you something, Edward—preachers blow their brains out too. Don't think they don't. The best preachers simply turn into undertakers and shoot themselves. Believe me.
(*He smiles.*)
But I've taken the revolver out of the box, Edward. It's silver.
(*Slowly he shuts one eye, holds the revolver at arm's length and aims it at the door, then lowers it and in both hands, holding the box on his knees, inspects it closely.*)
It's going to make a loud noise. You better plug your ears.

EDWARD:

What's the matter? What's the matter with you, Papa?

# THE UNDERTAKER

**FATHER:**

> (*raising the revolver over his head and again aiming it at the door*)

There's nothing the matter with me, of course. I've always been fond of you—despite your weight. I've always been as fond of you as I once was of a little black dog I discovered in a field of red clay near the Negro church. You know the church, Edward. It's where the chickens always block the road if you're out driving. At any rate, my little black dog approached me on its belly with its fat paws outspread and its grinning snout pushing along in the red clay and its tail thumping and its eyes turned up to mine—its belly was as flat and gray and wide as a distended bladder of some kind, Edward—and that miserable salivating animal seemed to know it was my destiny. A Negro dog, obviously, with my own fate in its belly and in its glistening eyes, because as soon as it reached my feet, with its heart pounding and its stump of a tail beating the damp bloody clay and its little teeth coming loose in its wormy gums, it rolled over. It rolled over, Edward, and dangled its fat dirty paws in the damp air and twisted its little black pear-shaped head so its eyes were fixed on mine and then, wriggling and trembling and groveling at my feet, Edward, it began to cry. I can tell you that that dog's voice was the only human voice I've ever heard—except yours, of course, and your mother's—and there was nothing to do but squat down then and there and rub my own white hand over that dog's flatulent gray

belly, which felt more like the warm skin of a gigantic rat than the tender hide of a miserable dog. And do you know what I knew, Edward, squatting there in the dampness and rubbing my poor dog's belly and knotted ears and the slimy pouches in the joints of its legs? I knew that that dog had been born in a dead litter, Edward, and that I was fond of it. I was fond of your mother, Edward—she was a princess—and I have been as fond of you as I was of the dog. That's real devotion, Edward—never let anyone tell you different. That's real innocence, my boy, true purity, true love. But I was separated from that devoted dog even while I was infecting my hand with the touch of its urgent skin—that was part of the beauty of it, Edward—and I've always been separated from you in the same way. So there's nothing the matter with me, Edward. I'm a man of cold principle and strong compassion. It's just that we've reached the moment when I must make our separation real. The Negroes were singing in the church when I met the dog. And now I am going to fire this gun for the sake of that dog. Do you understand? Do you?
(*He listens.*)
Are you there, Edward? Did you hear me? Speak to me, Edward.
(*He listens.*)
I'm warning you. I'll load the revolver if you don't.
(*He lowers the revolver and stares at it as if he hasn't seen it before.*)

EDWARD:

>(*pausing, raising his head*)
>Don't worry, Papa. I'm going to help you.

FATHER:

>What? What's that you say?

EDWARD:

>(*rising softly to his feet*)
>I'm going to save you, Papa.

FATHER:

>Nonsense. You haven't been listening to me. You haven't been paying attention.

EDWARD:

>Wait, Papa, wait. I'm going to play my cello for you. I will play for you, poor Papa.

FATHER:

>No, no, never mind. . . . It will do no good. . . . Do you hear me? No good. . . .

(*Edward holds out his hand as if to speak, then thinks better of it, smiles, and turns and exits silently stage right. Father scowls, hurriedly wipes his face with the handkerchief.*)

>Not the cello, Edward. Please.
>(*He listens.*)
>I forbid you, Edward. I do not want to hear that cello ever again. Do you understand?
>(*He listens.*)
>Are you there?
>(*He rises silently and steps to the door, for a mo-*

*ment puts his ear to the door and then abruptly faces it.*)
Edward! Answer me!
(*He scowls and listens, unconsciously raises the revolver as if to ward off a blow.*)
This is no time to taunt me, Edward. I will not be an object of mockery.
(*He stares at the door, listens, seems to collapse, lets his arm fall to his side.*)
Edward? Edward?
(*He listens.*)
You won't answer.
(*He grimaces, licks his lips, dabs at his brow with the handkerchief.*)
All right then, I'm going to load the revolver. I'm going to load the revolver this minute, Edward.
(*He listens, then slowly moves to the sink, stares into it, raises his head and removes the shaving brush from the mug and stands it upright on the shelf, then turns, leans back heavily against the sink and, dangling the revolver in full view, faces the door.*)
I should have done it sooner. I should have done it the day you were born. Then your mother could have held the three-weeks-old baby on her lap in the parlor—in the cool dark funeral parlor, my boy —and the Negroes could have come to pay condolences. They could have put that damn dog beside my body in the casket—that's where he belonged. But it's not too late, Edward. Do you hear?
(*He reaches out casually and places the revolver on the table.*)

It's not too late, my boy. The little shards of bone from your father's temple will be scattered around this lavatory floor like the bloody roots and broken crowns of extracted teeth. Or like bits of broken glass. Or like crushed shells washed up on the tide. Do you hear me, Edward? Scattered like little hard unrecognizable bright particles in the sawdust of an empty butcher's shop.
(*He listens.*)
You can crouch out there if you want to, Edward, and refuse to talk to your father on his dying day. You may deny me your voice if you want to, Edward. But I know what I'm talking about—the sound of this shot will kill everything. Everything. Your dream, your mother, my Negroes, my dog—everything. It will all be gone, Edward, all of it. No cheek, beard, toilet water, no signs of the undertaker. Everything will be gone—except you, of course. Nothing could kill you, Edward. Not even me. Do you hear? Do you comprehend what I'm saying, at last?

(*Edward enters awkwardly, quickly, silently, from stage right, holding a bow and carrying an old cello in his arms. He reaches the lavatory steps and, as quietly as possible, stands the cello on the floor, positions it, raises the bow high and readies himself to play.*)

Edward? Is that you?
(*He snatches up the revolver and box, sits belligerently on the toilet lid and holds the box on his lap, aims the revolver unsteadily at the door.*)

You heard it all, Edward, didn't you. Heard it all and refused to talk to your poor father. Left me alone in silence to break the seal by myself. Well, we'll see, Edward. We'll see how you bear this silence in later years.
(*He listens.*)
Edward! Stop scratching at the door of my tomb and speak to me . . . !

(*Lights grow dim in the lavatory while a spotlight slowly fixes Edward in a soft glow.*)

**EDWARD:**
(*waving the bow above his head*)
Now, Papa. . . . Now I am going to play!

(*Father gasps, jumps, clutches his stomach, drops the box so that the bullets are scattered profusely and hopelessly about the lavatory floor. Still holding the revolver, he stares down at the bullets, slips to his knees on the floor, crouches, but is unable to move and merely turn his bewildered and angry face toward the door. Fervently but clumsily Edward plays a rhapsodic melody on his cello, while Father, after listening for a moment in anger and amazement, slowly climbs to his feet, grips the edge of the sink and, suddenly, begins to declaim above the sound of the music.*)

**FATHER:**
Go thou thy way, and I go mine;
   Apart, yet not afar,
Only a thin veil hangs between
   The pathways where we are. . . .

I know not where thy road may lie,
   Or which way mine will be;
If mine will lead thro' parching sands,
   And thine beside the sea. . . .
I sigh, sometimes, to see thy face
   But since this may not be,
I'll leave thee. . . .
(*He breaks off his recitation.*)
Edward! Edward, stop it!

(*Edward ceases his playing, bow in midair, and Father takes a step from the sink.*)

I've dropped the bullets.
(*He kneels, begins to gather them up, reaching beneath the tub, etc.*)
It's your fault, Edward. I dropped them because of you.

(*Edward remains frozen, holding the cello upright and the bow still in midair. Father rises, holding a handful of bullets in his outstretched cupped palm.*)

**EDWARD:**

Papa, wait! I'm not finished. . . .

**FATHER:**

(*dropping the bullets into the tub*)
There you go again. Can't you keep quiet?

(*Slowly Edward lays down cello and bow and kneels on the first lavatory step. Father picks up a single bullet, holds high the revolver and inserts the bullet into the chamber. Then he steps to the door. Lights fade almost to dark on Father and Edward.*)

Edward! I have unlocked the door. There is no point in making someone break down the door to get me....

(*Sounds of the cello are heard offstage. Father, dimly seen, turns and sits on the toilet lid, holds the revolver in his lap.*)

EDWARD:
>(*in darkness*)
>But may I come in then, Papa? Oh Papa....

(*The stage goes to total darkness.*)

FATHER:
>Goodby, Edward....

(*A strong steady light infuses the lavatory, revealing Father with the revolver at right angles to his temple, then slowly fades. The sounds of the cello rise in the darkness, but they cease when a spotlight reveals Edward standing at stage right. He yawns, loosens his tie, pulls a handkerchief from his coat pocket and wipes his brow.*)

EDWARD:
>A hot day in summer. A hot day in the middle of July. Hot as the devil. I wish there was a muffler tied around my neck and beating in the wind, old man. And a white driving cap on my head and driving goggles over my eyes, by God.
>(*A warm light rises in the empty lavatory as he strolls to the steps and mounts them.*)

Give me a fine old yellow antique automobile and it wouldn't take me a minute to drive off the face of the earth like you, old man.
(*He removes his suitcoat, hangs it on the rack, removes his tie and rolls up his sleeves.*)
But you didn't get so very far after all, my poor old friend. And here I am, still turning on the tap that couldn't save your life....
(*He turns it on.*)
still splashing this water on the skin of my face.
(*He splashes his face, with his fingers wipes the water from his eyes.*)
I've listened to you for thirty years. I still find bits of your angry ending in the linoleum or behind the tub—the Indianheads of my childhood, old man.
(*He picks up the shaving mug and brush, studies them, puts them down.*)
For thirty years I've wanted to shout with pleasure when July rolls around, wanted to shout and rub my own wet tongue and lips against your dog and your Negroes and your silent revolver. For thirty years I've laughed at the sight of you trapped like a black fish between this bathtub and that old white singing toilet. All this time you've lived inside me, with your mockery and jokes.... All this time you've been the rusty fishhook lodged inside my brain.
(*He seizes the shaving mug, fills it with water, faces stage right.*)
So come on, old man—I'm waiting.

(*He drinks.*)
Let's get it over with.

(*He listens intently, smiles, and in answer there comes, from offstage, the loud angry sound of a single shot, as the lights fade and sounds of the cello drift faintly across the stage.*)

**CURTAIN**

# THE QUESTIONS

The Questions *was first performed as an experimental production by the Stanford Repertory Theater, January 13–16, 1966, under the direction of Robert Loper. The Man was played by Glenn Cannon and The Young Girl was played by Carol Androsky.*

*A massive dark wooden armchair in a white setting so neutral and shadowed that it might be courtroom, doctor's office, sun parlor, or the pure space of psychic activity. An old-fashioned ceiling fan turns slowly and with a loud humming noise above the chair.*

THE MAN.

THE YOUNG GIRL.

*Lights up on the girl seated in the chair and the man standing stage right with his back to her.*

MAN:
>Sit up straight and try to—pay attention. Please.
>(*He waits while the girl obeys.*)
>And you're going to concentrate on the hair problem. You're going to try not to chew your hair. Remember?

(*The girl arranges her hair and smiles at the back of the man's head.*)

>Now—about the dream. . . .

GIRL:
>Papa's dream?

MAN:
>Yes. Your father's—nightmare.

GIRL:
>Well, to me it was embarrassing—you know—but Mama and Adrian said it was just silly.

MAN:
>Wasn't it thoughtless of your father to tell his dream in public? Wouldn't you say it was—indiscreet?

GIRL:
>Papa didn't tell us the dream, of course. Mama did. Papa's wonderful with the tea things and really beautiful when he wanders around whistling to him-

self or strolls in the garden with his hands in his pockets.

(*The man removes his hands from his pockets, smiles, reaches for his handkerchief.*)

But Papa's pretty adamant about indiscretion. He'd have a fit before he'd do anything indiscreet.

MAN:

Perhaps it was unintentional. Perhaps he blurted out his dream by mistake. Isn't your father capable of human fallibility like other men?

GIRL:

Well sure. But you're barking up the wrong tree. I told you—he wasn't there. It was just Mama and Adrian and me.

MAN:

He was whistling to himself in the house while the three of you were drinking tea in the garden?

GIRL:

He was having his riding lesson. Anyhow, he wasn't there.

MAN:

Riding lesson?
(*He smiles, wipes his face.*)
But how do you know he was having his—riding lesson? How do you know he wasn't hiding behind the rose arbor all the while and listening to the recitation of his—silly dream?

**GIRL:**

What's the matter with you? He fell off twice that afternoon and broke his glasses. He showed me.

**MAN:**

Not much good at riding but excellent at the tea table—is that it?

**GIRL:**

You know—it took him years to learn to post and he always had trouble with the stirrups. He just couldn't find his seat.
(*She pretends to post in the chair.*)

**MAN:**

Repeat that, please.

**GIRL:**

You mean—he couldn't find his seat? Well, he couldn't. You can't ride a horse without a good seat.

**MAN:**

No doubt your father was a man of courage as well as determination. He must have been brave to spend his life falling off. . . .

**GIRL:**

Gunpowder.

**MAN:**

Yes, Gunpowder.

**GIRL:**

The mighty chestnut, part Percheron and part race horse, a classical hunter and best in the county. . . .

MAN:
> Yes, the best in the county. But your father certainly must have been brave to spend his life falling off this Gunpowder for the sake of your mother.

GIRL:
> He wouldn't quit, that's for sure.

MAN:
> Such courage is reprehensible—don't you think?

GIRL:
> I never thought it was—reprehensible....

MAN:
> Please, take the hair out of your mouth.
> (*He pauses while the girl obeys.*)
> Didn't your father and mother give you any moral training?
> (*He smiles, wipes his face.*)
> Or what about Adrian? Didn't he at least give you a little instruction in the spiritual arts?

GIRL:
> Adrian said Papa was a joke.

MAN:
> Adrian said that. You're sure?

GIRL:
> Yes. And Mama said the only service Papa was good for was the tea service.

MAN:
> Your mother said that.

GIRL:
> Yes. It was one of her dirty jokes.

MAN:
> But rather obvious and harmless—don't you think?

GIRL:
> I guess it's just a dirty joke. You know....

MAN:
> The tea service....
> (*laughing briefly*)
> not bad. Not bad.
> (*He wipes his face and scowls.*)
> It appears that your father was a lover of animals and lover of good tea. Use your head now—there's a lot at stake.

GIRL:
> (*smiling at the back of the man's head*)
> Well, he might have been a ninny over that awful Gunpowder—always trying to prove himself, as Mama said—and that dream of his was sort of embarrassing, like Mama's joke. You know—sort of pathetic. But he made tea Japanese style, and that's an art. Papa in his red silk blazer and going through this tea ritual like a Japanese, but using the big old silver tray and silver pot his own Mama shoved up the chimney in their house in Charleston—can you imagine?
> (*She chews her hair, curls up in the chair, smiles at the back of the man's head.*)
> He was just beautiful, that's all.

MAN:

> The old house in Charleston.... Now we're getting somewhere.

GIRL:

> Can you imagine?

MAN:

> There was something about a name cut into an upstairs windowpane with a diamond ring....

GIRL:

> And a hundred-year-old buggy hung up under the roof of the barn where they used to play kissing games....
> (*She shuts her eyes and imitates the kisses.*)

MAN:

> Young woman.... Please.

GIRL:

> And don't forget the old red pony and the little pond covered with scum....

MAN:

> And the tea service.... The large tray with solid silver grapes around the edges, and leaves of course —leaves as small as the palm of your grandmother's hand. And then the pot, that enormous pot with its fluted spout and host of little fat silver cherubim reflecting the heat of the tea water itself, and the tongs and the bowl and the creamer and a white napkin....

GIRL:

> Scones. Don't forget the scones. . . .

MAN:

> (*smiling*)
> Yes. That's right. But no doubt your father baked the scones himself. That's true, isn't it?

GIRL:

> Well, sure he did. You know. He got a kick out of using the oven. But don't get the wrong idea. . . .

MAN:

> We are doing our best, young woman. After all, there is a life at stake.

GIRL:

> Well, you better watch out. Scones don't prove a thing. Neither does Mama's joke.

(*The man smiles.*)

> Go ahead and smile. It's OK with me. Papa was just beautiful, that's all.

MAN:

> I'm sure he appreciates your loyalty.

GIRL:

> You bet he does.

MAN:

> I'm sure he returns your—affection.

GIRL:

> Just don't make a "thing" out of it. OK?

**MAN:**

> I must ask you to sit up properly and stop chewing your hair. Can't you concentrate? I should warn you that this girlish display merely puts your father in a worse light.

(*The girl shifts her position but again stares warmly at the back of the man's head.*)

> That's better. Now, about the dream—describe it again, please, as briefly and simply as you can.

**GIRL:**

> You want me to just tell it in my own words . . . ?

**MAN:**

> In your own words.

**GIRL:**

> Well, then, Papa was over knocking himself out with Gunpowder, like I said . . . .

**MAN:**

> Making a ninny of himself with the horse, to use your word.

**GIRL:**

> . . . . really knocking himself out trying to ride hell for leather into these little two-foot jumps, and Mama and Adrian and I were trying to cool off under the pear trees where Trushka was licking her new pups. . . .

**MAN:**

> Your father had seen the pups, of course?

GIRL:

> He didn't know they were born yet. Anyhow, Mama picked up one of the pups and was letting it nuzzle her blouse—you know—and that's when Adrian started the whole thing.

MAN:

> How? How did he start it?

GIRL:

> Well, he smiled for a long time and watched the dog crawling on Mama, and then suddenly he put his drink on the grass and leaned forward and winked and told the dog it wouldn't get anything. That's all. I mean, do you understand?

MAN:

> Yes, we understand. Go on.

GIRL:

> It was nothing, you see. But Mama laughed and told Adrian he better not be too sure about that, and went over and knelt down and gave the puppy back to Trushka. . . .

MAN:

> And buttoned her blouse.
> (*Pause*)
> She buttoned her blouse then, did she not?

GIRL:

> It zipped. The white silk blouse with the monogram near the collar and the zipper in back? You know . . . . from that little shop in Cantigny?

MAN:

    Yes, yes. Go on.

GIRL:

    Well, the puppy found his way to the table with the rest of his little brothers and sisters, as Adrian said, and Mama leaned back and put her hands behind her head and smiled—like this (*She imitates the action.*)—and shut her eyes, I think, and began to talk.

MAN:

    Excuse me. It was hot and she had been drinking and you were all feeling a little careless and were— acting like children. So far so good. Now what did she say?

GIRL:

    (*slowly, imitating her mother*)
    He has had a dream. Can you imagine? He dreams that he and I are attending a party and that I am talking with a group of men on the other side of the room in my bra. Shoes, stockings, skirt, hat, jewelry, a glass to my lips—you understand—but nothing else on top except the bra. It's so obvious, isn't it. Nothing happens. Nothing at all. It's obvious, it's irritating, it's amusing, it's silly—but to him it's painful. What can I do?

(*For the first time the man turns and stares at the girl, who opens her eyes, sits up, shakes loose her hair, meets the man's gaze and laughs.*)

    That's Mama, all right. That's the way she is.

MAN:

> A very composed person. The kind of woman who can tell dreams.

GIRL:

> And dirty jokes.

MAN:

> You said she studied Greek. . . .

GIRL:

> Of course she did. Scholastic and athletic and passionate—that's Mama. Adrian said she was a nude *glacée*. But Mama said she just lived directly and for only one purpose—to make up her mind.

MAN:

> An admirable ambition. . . .

GIRL:

> But she couldn't make up her mind about Papa's dream. I mean, she didn't know how to handle it.

MAN:

> We might say your mother came a cropper over your father's dream.

GIRL:

> It was a problem, all right. It was embarrassing— you know. But then Mama just lifted her skirt a little—like this (*She lifts her skirt.*)—and laughed and said she thought it would be better if Papa dreamed about her legs instead of her bra.

(*The man stares at the girl's legs and then turns away.*)

It sounded like a good idea. It was the most natural thing in the world. But then Mama gave up and admitted she couldn't tell Papa what to dream about. (*She lowers her skirt and looks away.*)

MAN:

And while this conversation was taking place in the garden, your father was three miles away on Gunpowder's back with his arms around the horse's neck. Am I correct?

GIRL:

Well, no. He had already fallen off twice, you see, and broken his glasses. So by this time Gunpowder was already in his stall and Papa was trying to get him to eat some grain out of his cupped palm.

MAN:

Your father was still trying to—make friends?

GIRL:

He hated Gunpowder. He always did.

MAN:

And Adrian, who was from . . . .

GIRL:

Liverpool.

MAN:

That's right. Liverpool. One of those small common dark-haired self-educated men from Liverpool, as you put it. Did your father hate Adrian as well? After all, Adrian called your mother a nude *glacée*.

GIRL:

There you go again. The wrong tree. Papa didn't *know* about the nude *glacée* business. But it wouldn't have made any difference. Papa liked Adrian. Papa said Adrian looked like a mechanic and waved his Webley in the air when he got drunk. You know—Adrian was in the war and Papa wasn't. Anyhow, Papa told Adrian to hang around.

MAN:

And what was your mother's attitude toward this man from Liverpool?

GIRL:

She didn't care for him.

MAN:

Young woman. Don't you realize what you're saying?

GIRL:

Well, she told him Papa's dream.

MAN:

And isn't that "caring for him"?

GIRL:

Adrian's remark to the puppy reminded Mama of the dream, that's all. It was on her mind.

MAN:

But don't you think that episode in the garden was an act of confidence, an act of supreme intimacy?

**GIRL:**

Every minute of Mama's life was intimate. You know.

**MAN:**

You mean her life was—unruffled.

**GIRL:**

She was just serene, that's all.

**MAN:**

And passionate.

**GIRL:**

She was, a sexual person, obviously. But she never dreamed. She didn't want to dream. She said she wasn't going to lose herself in dreams, like Papa.

**MAN:**

Doesn't it occur to you that your mother might have been driven by despair? That your father might have been a kind of sweet tooth gone rotten in the healthy flesh of your mother's life? Doesn't it occur to you that your mother might have wanted to hold Adrian's hand in the garden and that your father really hated Adrian, despite the—evidence?

**GIRL:**

She did hold his hand.

**MAN:**

She did?

**GIRL:**

Well, sure. What else could she do? Mama said—Here he comes (Papa was chugging up the drive in the old ranch wagon), so the three of us started for the house, holding hands. That's when Mama waved and told Papa to go and have a look at the dogs.

MAN:
    And when you ran to him, your father's words were (*imitating father*)—Broke another pair of glasses.... Is that correct?

(*The girl nods, kneels impulsively in the chair.*)

    And your own words were....

GIRL:
    How's the posting?

MAN:
    Haven't quite got the hang of it yet. But there's something wrong with that horse. Something wrong with his legs....

GIRL:
    Poor Papa, you've torn your jacket. I can practically see your shoulder blade.... Trushka's beautiful with the pups, come see.... She wasn't due for a week, but there they are....

(*The man glances briefly at the girl, turns away.*)

    All five of them....

MAN:
    Well, now, those are damn fine pups. Take it from the old Master of Hounds himself.
    (*Pause*)

GIRL:

>The Master of Hounds business was a joke.

MAN:

>(*wiping his face*)
>He was a humorous man, your father. Humorous and reprehensible.
>(*Pause*)

GIRL:

>I want a cigarette.

MAN:

>You'll have to wait.

GIRL:

>Just a few puffs—please?

MAN:

>And you must sit properly in the chair until we're done.

GIRL:

>(*sitting and plucking at the arm of the chair*)
>Anyway, that's wrong about Papa hating Adrian. Papa couldn't ride, but at least he was in on the kill with Adrian. You know—they did it together.

MAN:

>Yes. Your father was in on the kill. We'll come to that. But first . . . . (*slowly*) how did your father know that your mother discussed his dream with Adrian?

GIRL:

> She didn't discuss the dream, she didn't make a "thing" out of it.

MAN:

> How did your father know?

GIRL:

> I told him.

MAN:

> You told him.

(*The girl nods, plucks at the arm of the chair.*)

> When did you tell him?

GIRL:

> I want a cigarette.

MAN:

> When did you tell him?

GIRL:

> You know—I just told him, down there looking at Trushka's litter.

MAN:

> But why?

(*The girl shakes her head.*)

> You thought he needed to know about this—betrayal?

(*Again the girl shakes her head.*)

> You thought he should reconsider his feelings about Adrian, is that it?
> (*Pause*)

Why, then? Did you simply want to share his confidence? No? Then perhaps you wanted him to choose his audiences more carefully. You were being thoughtful.
(*Pause*)
Or maybe you were just trying to get a rise out of him. Is that it? You couldn't have meant to hurt your father, who was a kind and humorous Charleston man with a nagging dream. So maybe you were just trying to get a rise out of him.
(*Pause*)
Answer the question.

GIRL:

(*smiling*)
I don't know. But it didn't make any difference. He didn't care.

(*The man turns and stares at the girl.*)

MAN:

That's your opinion—that he didn't care?

GIRL:

Well, sure.

MAN:

And how did you reach this—conclusion?

GIRL:

It didn't mean anything to Mama and me and Adrian, so how could it have meant anything to him? You know—Adrian said that if it had been his dream there wouldn't have been any bra in it, so

you can see how much it meant to Adrian. And another thing—when I told Papa, he just puckered his lips and made a lot of little kissing noises and said the smallest dog was going to be the best. You see?
(*Pause*)

MAN:

The word you used was—embarrassing.

GIRL:

OK—embarrassing.

MAN:

And according to your own statement, your mother's word was—painful.

GIRL:

OK—painful.

MAN:

Yet now you say he didn't care. Do you think you might have been mistaken?

GIRL:

Papa has feelings. He's not a child. But Papa's theory was that some emotions are just hunches and others are little black ugly bats you can crush with your teeth. And these were just hunches. So it was all right. Don't you see?

(*The man slowly turns his back to the girl.*)

Anyhow, I didn't get a rise out of him, which proves the point.
(*Pause*)

MAN:
> Your mother was holding hands in the garden.

GIRL:
> I told you—we all were.

MAN:
> Your mother held hands with Adrian willingly—did she not?

GIRL:
> Papa said you'd never know Mama had a golden flank by the looks of her, but that you could sure tell she was a woman by her hands. She kept her nails trimmed short so she could ride—you know—but she worked on the cuticles, and the backs of her hands really smelled of the sun. Papa said Mama's small size and riding get-up couldn't fool anyone, and that obviously Mama was Artemis and not just another horsy woman in the hunting field, and that obviously she got the power in her hands from drawing the bow and not just from pulling on the reins all day. Her hands were strong but—you know—relaxed.

MAN:
> And your mother—this goddess—gave her hand to Adrian. Did she not?

GIRL:
> I told you. We heard the car and we jumped up and I caught Adrian's hand and Mama's hand was—there. She wasn't a goddess, she was a person. And

she wasn't Desdemona, either. She knew what she was doing and she kept her handkerchief in her pocket, where it belonged. Don't worry. She was a smart person. But if you want to know, what she was really like was a nun. Except for her jokes and horsemanship and feeling for Papa and the celibacy business, she might have been a nun. But when I told Adrian, he said Mama wasn't born for a wimple. That's all *he* knew. Now give me a cigarette. And can't you get anything more out of that terrible old fan? It's hot in here.

MAN:

(*clasping his hands behind his back*)
How did your mother become—involved with Adrian?

GIRL:

Why can't I smoke?

MAN:

(*slowly*)
How did your mother become—involved with him?

GIRL:

She wasn't involved with him. She didn't care for him.

MAN:

You insist on that.

GIRL:

She didn't like his war stories. You know. She didn't like his accent. She didn't like his eyes or the smell of his breath. And she wasn't sure he had a reason for living.

MAN:

Young woman, your mother didn't talk to this man and hold his hand and spend her time in his presence for nothing.

GIRL:

I'm not a child.

MAN:

Then what are you hiding?

GIRL:

Well, heavens, it was perfectly open. There was nothing clandestine about Mama or Papa or Adrian —or me. We weren't—secretive.

MAN:

Continue.

GIRL:

There were three perfectly good reasons why Mama didn't kick him out....

MAN:

(*smiling*)
Name them, please.

GIRL:

For Papa's sake.

(*The man nods.*)

And because he came to us bathed in blood.

(*The man nods again and smiles broadly.*)

And because he told Mama he was going to leave a mark on her soul.

(*The man turns abruptly, crosses to stage left and faces the girl.*)

Well, what could she do? She couldn't kick him out after he said that. It must have been like Papa's dream. Sort of—embarrassing, and sort of—pleasurable. There was nothing she could do but wait.
(*Pause*)

MAN:

(*slowly*)
How did they meet?

GIRL:

He fell off his horse and Mama helped him. That's all.

MAN:

Is that all? The men in your mother's life had something in common, wouldn't you say?

GIRL:

Well, no. Papa was a ninny about horses, whereas Adrian turned out to be a little knight from Liverpool. Papa just slopped off, you see, because he had no seat. But Adrian had been a gentleman jockey, or so he claimed (because that's when Mama smiled and said—Jockey, perhaps, but you're no gentleman) and when Adrian fell off he always tried to pull the horse down with him. Anyhow, the meeting between Mama and Adrian was dramatic.

MAN:

It must have been, if he—marked her soul.

GIRL:

That was later.

MAN:

Then you have no firsthand information about the "drama" of their meeting.

GIRL:

I was there, that's all. I mean, Mama came back for Old Sam and then drove off lickety-split in the ranch wagon and then brought him home and Papa shouted....

MAN:

(*turning downstage*)
For God's sake, get the first-aid kit!

GIRL:

That's right. But Sam already had the first-aid kit. Mama kept it in the car.

MAN:

Your mother was a—deliberate woman.

GIRL:

She was just lucid. She lived directly. Anyhow, she stayed upstairs for about an hour and then joined us for tea on the veranda, and Papa asked her if the man was hurt.

MAN:

Your father was—curious.

## THE QUESTIONS

**GIRL:**

Well, sure he was. He watched her a minute and then he said . . . .

**MAN:**

At least you've dipped your hands in the blood of a man, this time, instead of in the blood of a helpless animal.

(*He smiles.*)

**GIRL:**

That's right. Papa didn't think much of hunting foxes. Anyhow, Mama glanced at him and smiled and began to talk. She said the horse was hurt. She said the horse was lacerated but she thought he'd live.

**MAN:**

Her exact words, please. If you remember them.

**GIRL:**

(*as at the tea table*)

I was walking Cavalier by the creek when a riderless horse crashed through the thicket on the other side, shot me a look of pure murder, forded the creek with stirrups flying and charged as if he meant to run us down. I urged Cavalier into him, but of course poor Cavalier went wild and swerved. It took me a good quarter mile to catch that runaway. He was black with sweat and badly lacerated and covered with blood. Obviously his rider had been whipping him deliberately into the trees. I changed mounts and went back to find the rider.

He had more blood on him than the horse. Then I returned for Sam. You'll be happy to know that horse and rider will both live. We won't have any deaths on our hands. But that man has the most unpleasant English accent I've ever heard.
(*Pause*)
Wasn't she wonderful? You know—if everyone could have lived as directly as Mama, I might not be sitting here this way. I might not have seen the tryst that time and heard about the dream and prayed for Papa.

MAN:
(*pausing*)
You prayed for your father?

GIRL:
You know—I tried.

MAN:
But why?

GIRL:
I just wanted Papa to be in on the kill.
(*The man turns and faces the girl.*)
I thought it didn't work—the praying—but I guess it did. I mean, if you want things to happen, I guess they do.

MAN:
(*turning abruptly downstage*)
What did your mother propose to do with this—injured man?

GIRL:

> Well, Mama said they would have to feed him and then Papa could drive him home in the ranch wagon and she'd follow on the horse. But Papa said this fellow from Liverpool was a gift from the gods and he wasn't going to let him get away so easily. Mama shrugged.

MAN:

> And you yourself saw him for the first time that afternoon, did you not?

GIRL:

> (*smiling*)
> Mama and Papa were resting—at least I thought they were resting—and I was sitting out by the little iron nigger with a ring in his fist, when I heard a noise and looked up and found him right there smiling at me. I smiled back—you know—and he pointed at the little iron nigger and said . . . .

MAN:

> Let's go riding with him, what do you say?

GIRL:

> (*laughing*)
> That's right. And I was ready, you know. For a minute I really saw the two of us with the little black iron figure of the boy jogging along between us on a mule or something.

MAN:

> And did you think that this man from Liverpool was a—gift from the gods?

GIRL:

    Well, no. But he was wonderful. He looked like Hitler. He was wearing black boots with brown tops and white twill britches and a black turtleneck sweater. No wonder Papa liked him. He was attractive.

MAN:

    (*facing downstage*)
    But you still believe that he was not attractive to—your mother.

GIRL:

    She rescued him. She brought him home. She fixed him up. She approved of the way he rode. But she didn't like the sound of his voice—she told us that—and she said his jokes were dirtier than her own.

MAN:

    But you, at least, thought he would make a good riding companion that afternoon.

GIRL:

    Well, sure I did. But just when I thought he was going to bring the little iron nigger boy to life, why there was Papa shouting at us from the doorway. . . .

MAN:

    Quit talking to the hired hand, sir, and come in and meet the master. . . .

GIRL:

    That's right. Papa always called me the hired hand. Anyhow, we went inside and they shook hands and Papa said . . . .

MAN:
> We've been waiting for you, Adrian. Now we can get going with our little *ménage-à-trois*.

GIRL:
> And it turned out that Mama was standing at the head of the stairs, because she laughed and said— You gentlemen may do whatever you like about this *ménage-à-trois*, but take care of yourselves, because I'm not going to mother either one of you.
> (*Pause*)
> Can't you put a little pep into that fan? And I'd like a drink. May I have a drink of water?
> (*Pause*)
> It's the *ménage-à-trois*, isn't it. Now you're going to bark up that tree awhile, so I can't have my cigarette or a drink of water.
> (*Pause*)

MAN:
> You said your father was never—indiscreet.

GIRL:
> Well, heavens, it was a perfectly innocent remark.

MAN:
> An objective observer would call it indiscreet.

GIRL:
> Well, it wasn't. I told you Papa wanted him around. Papa was being lucid for once, don't you see? That's just what we were—I mean, I didn't count, of course—but that's what they were. It didn't mean anything.

MAN:

>Until the tryst. You said yourself that there was a tryst.

GIRL:

>Well, OK, there was the tryst. But that didn't mean anything either—except to me.
>(*She chews her hair.*)

MAN:

>(*slowly crossing to stage right*)
>How long ago, exactly, did the events of this day take place? How long ago did your meeting with Adrian occur?

GIRL:

>Three years.

MAN:

>(*slowly*)
>Three years?

GIRL:

>Mama leaned on the pitchfork—she enjoyed working in the barn with Old Sam—and looked at me and looked at Adrian. And then she said—I married late and I am the mother of a fourteen-year-old girl, and anyone around here will tell you I am not easily impressed. I am not mysterious and I am not bored. Sam can back me up on that. Can't you, Sam?
>(*Pause*)
>So it was three years.

MAN:

> And all this time they were living together—your mother and father and Adrian—without rupture or regret or antagonism. Is that correct?

GIRL:

> Well, heavens, they weren't living together. Adrian was a person of independent means. He just came and went, that's all.

MAN:

> You know what I intended by the phrase, do you not?

GIRL:

> OK—living together. What's the difference? Your words don't mean any more or less than mine.
> (*Pause*)
> You know—Mama and Adrian would start out for a ride and Papa would shout....

MAN:

> Don't get off the horses, you two!

GIRL:

> Or Papa would wheel the tea service onto the veranda and frown and say....

MAN:

> Smack her on the rump, Adrian. It's the only thing these country women understand.

GIRL:

> You see? That's all it meant. And don't start that indiscretion business—please. Because Papa knew

that the essence of vulgarity is the lack of charity. And Papa was charitable. You know—he was only pure. He always said he married Mama because her handwriting matched the writing on the windowpane in the house in Charleston.

MAN:

Young woman. Suppose we assume that your father knew perfectly well that your mother would not get off her horse when she was alone with Adrian, and that Adrian would not strike your mother's rump under any circumstances. And suppose we assume that your father knew perfectly well that your mother and Adrian would have liked nothing better than to do these things. Might we not then question the propriety of the kind of thing your father was apparently compelled to say?

GIRL:

(*smiling*)
Well, heavens. How could he know?

(**Pause. The man faces the girl.**)

MAN:

How can you consider the possible consequences of all this—consequences such as death, grief, anguish, a life of emotional oblivion—and not cooperate?

GIRL:

You sound like an old judge or something. You sound like Papa in a bad mood. Papa always pretended he was a maniac when he was in a bad mood. When he was angry he claimed he was the son of John Wilkes Booth. Sometimes I thought he was really trying to frighten me and make me cry. Is that what you're trying to do? Is it my fault there's nothing to cry about? You know—it isn't fair. Here I am telling you my life and you say I'm not cooperating. It's just not fair.

(*The man takes a step toward the girl, who smiles slightly, slowly rubs her arms, shifts in the chair, arranges her skirt, then smiles radiantly at the man.*)

OK, I'll try. I'll be lots more cooperative. I really will. I'll tell you just what you want to know. OK?

(*The man turns downstage.*)

Give me a chance. OK?

(*The man walks to the edge of the stage, wipes his face.*)

How about the tryst? I bet you'd like to hear about the tryst. It was full of indiscretion—really. It was the worst moment in my life. OK?

MAN:

(*slowly*)

I would like you to understand the seriousness of our discussion. I would like you to understand that what we are talking about is no different from any other prolonged relationship of this kind.

GIRL:

But it is different! Of course it's different.

MAN:

This affair is no less sordid than any other of its kind.

GIRL:
> You see? You have no right to use that word—affair.

MAN:
> Can you think of a word more suitable?

GIRL:
> I guess affair's OK. That's what it was. And I think maybe the tryst was sordid.
> (*Pause*)
> I guess it was.

MAN:
> Very well. Continue.

GIRL:
> I guess I'm like the girl who gets turned into a bird and has to sing forever just because of the messy life she was mixed up in. It's not much fun.

(*The man clears his throat.*)

> All right, all right. I'm trying.
> (*She sprawls in the chair, then slowly sits up, crosses her legs and studies the man.*)
> It was dark—naturally—and I woke up knowing the fan had stopped. I could see the four white blades standing still up there in the shadows, and I couldn't decide whether someone had sneaked in and turned it off or whether it had just quit.
> (*Pause*)
> After a while I got out of bed and felt the switch and discovered it had just quit. That fan never did

any good, of course—like this one (*She glances overhead.*)—but I didn't like it standing still that way. You know—I like things clicking right along in proper order. . . .

MAN:

This fan of yours—it was from the house in Charleston, is that correct?

GIRL:

The fan, the tea service, the little black iron nigger boy—they were Papa's contribution to the marriage, as Mama said. They all came from that old place down in Charleston.

MAN:

I see. His contribution . . . . Please go on.

GIRL:

There wasn't much to it, really. You know. Maybe I thought I'd meet Adrian out there, maybe I wanted to visit Sam's grave and scare myself to death. (Sam had died by then, of course. You know.) Anyhow, I went outside. . . .

MAN:

But it did not enter your head to do any—spying. Is that correct? You made no particular effort to be —stealthy. Or did you?

GIRL:

(*staring at the man, then recrossing her legs and leaning forward*)
I went outside and drifted around the house like a

little white moth, I guess, and naturally I hadn't gotten as far as the birdbath when I saw them—the man and women holding each other in their arms not twenty feet from Papa's favorite rhododendron tree. Well, heavens. You know. I thought it was wonderful. . . .

MAN:

So you decided to crouch down behind the birdbath and watch—is that what you did?

GIRL:

I just thought to myself—it may be improper, but I'm glad. I'm glad. I'm glad. . . .

MAN:

So you took up a position behind the birdbath where you could witness everything. . . .

GIRL:

I just thought to myself—that's my mother over there and she's really holding on to him. I'm glad, I'm glad, I'm glad. And I've got a right to see.

MAN:

(*turning to the girl*)
But in fact you had no such right. Do you understand?

GIRL:

So I began walking toward them. You know. Just walking.
(*Pause*)
Well, I knew they weren't kissing. If they had been

kissing before they must have stopped doing it by then. But they were standing there in a kind of passionate embrace....
(*She imitates the embrace.*)
you know—and I could tell they were smelling each other's hair and touching each other and smiling into each other's shoulders in the dark. It was wonderful....

MAN:

Perhaps wonderful. Perhaps despicable. But the fact of the matter is that you intruded—and in the very sight of your own father's favorite tree. Isn't that correct? You had no business outside, did you. But nonetheless you intruded on that scene—hypnotically. And even now you do not regret this intrusion of yours and appear to be incapable of feeling shame....
(*He glances at the girl, who merely watches him.*)
Wait, now. Control yourself.... Here, wipe your eyes.
(*He approaches the girl and gives her his handkerchief, which she accepts but does not use.*)
All right now. You witnessed this episode from beginning to end. Describe it, please.

GIRL:

(*her smile fading*)
That's all.

MAN:

You said that you were going to cooperate....

GIRL:
> But that's all.

MAN:
> I warn you, young woman....

GIRL:
> Well, heavens. It was Papa. Don't you see?

MAN:
> (*pausing*)
> I do not see. Explain yourself.

GIRL:
> Well, it was awful. As soon as he straightened up and I recognized him and realized Mama was having a tryst with her own husband and that it wasn't Adrian at all—well, that's when I must have had a taste of something sordid. Because that's when I got sick. You know—really sick. I just didn't like to see Papa standing out there in the middle of the night with his arms around Mama and his tweed jacket flung aside on the rhododendron tree. You know—it was sort of desperate. It made me sick. Who did Papa think he was, anyhow?

MAN:
> (*slowly*)
> Once again your judgment may have been wrong. Very wrong.

GIRL:
> It was the worst thing Papa ever did—embracing Mama out there like that—and it was the worst mo-

ment in my whole life. It was pathetic—don't you see?

**MAN:**

(*slowly*)
And that's all there was to it. Correct?

**GIRL:**

Well, heavens. I didn't hang around to see if there was going to be more. I'd seen enough. I had thought it was going to be Adrian, I guess I had really wanted it to be Adrian, I knew it would have been a lot better if it had been Adrian. Anyhow, I just walked back to the house and up to my room and tried to pray for Papa. And the next morning about five o'clock I was in the kitchen with Mama when Adrian came in and looked at her and said. . . .

**MAN:**

How about some of your instant pussy milk—the cats are raising Cain in the barn. . . .

**GIRL:**

That's right. It was one of his jokes. And a few hours later Papa decided to put a fresh coat of paint on the blackamoor—that's what he called the little black iron nigger boy—and of course we heard him shouting. . . .

**MAN:**

Come on out here, Adrian, and help me paint this damn blackamoor. . . .

**GIRL:**

That's right. Papa always liked to touch up the little black iron nigger boy with the ring in his fist. Papa used a bright and shiny stoveblacking for the skin and boots, and red enamel for the shirt and cap and nostrils, and white enamel for the britches and the whites of the eyes. I always enjoyed seeing Papa doing his art work—you know—and I was glad he could concentrate after what he'd been up to the night before. So I went outside with Adrian, who took one look at Papa and said. . . .

**MAN:**

Coo—your eyes are bloodshot. What's the matter with you anyway?

**GIRL:**

But Papa just waved at the glistening paint and said. . . .

**MAN:**

Don't worry your head about my eyes, Adrian. Just give me a hand with the eyes of this blasted blackamoor. Here—you paint one of them and I'll paint the other. What do you say?

**GIRL:**

But Adrian stuck his hands in his pockets and lifted his lip and winked at me and turned away, murmuring. . . .

**MAN:**

You Yanks are all the same—just up to the teeth with wit.

GIRL:

>And then Mama was leaning out the kitchen window and smiling, and I heard her say—That's Charleston humor, Adrian. Will you never learn?
>(*Pause*)
>And then Papa laughed and said. . . .

MAN:

>Don't pay any attention to what she says. She can't paint worth a damn.

GIRL:

>That's right. And then he dabbed away at his little blackamoor until noon. And finally he hung a sign from the iron ring: FRESH PAINT.
>(*Pause*)
>Well, you know. After Adrian came, the blackamoor, or little black iron nigger boy—whichever you want to call him—was just never the same again. You know—he had a little friendly life of his own. No wonder Papa kept him in such good shape. You know. . . .
>(*She recrosses her legs, swings her foot up and down, stares at the fan, etc.*)

MAN:

>(*staring at the girl until she sits still, then turning downstage*)
>Why didn't you tell your father you spied on him?

GIRL:

>There you go, trying to trap me again.
>(*She smiles*)

But, anyhow, the reason I didn't tell Papa I had seen the two of them together that night was because it was just pathetic. That's all. It was just one of those things I wanted to nurse along myself. OK?

MAN:

Did you feel sorry for your father—is that what you mean?

GIRL:

No. That's not what I mean. Being pathetic just doesn't have anything to do with feeling sorry. You know. I mean, I'd just never put the two of them in the same spot. There was just never anything to cry about—including Papa.

MAN:

But you prayed for your father? Didn't you pray for your father?

GIRL:

Well, sure I did.
(*Pause*)
But I bet you think I knelt beside the bed and joined my palms and raised my eyes to heaven or something. . . .

MAN:

I am not interested in the physical aspects of your efforts to pray.

GIRL:

Of course you're not. But it's just like what Adrian said about marking Mama's soul. I mean, you can use a word and make yourself understood without anyone believing literally in the word itself. You know—soul is practically meaningless, but in the context of Adrian and Mama it still comes at you like a little corkscrew of lightning from Thor himself. . . .

MAN:
Young woman. . . .

GIRL:
So when I said I prayed for Papa I only meant that I sat cross-legged at the foot of the bed and thought about him—to myself. I just sat there and cast my pebbles into the void—you know.

MAN:
Young woman, three years ago your mother brought home an injured man. . . .

GIRL:
With Sam's help. Don't forget Old Sam was in the picture too.

MAN:
. . . . brought home an injured man, and had him carried upstairs to her own room, and stayed alone with him for an hour. Is that correct?

GIRL:
(*pausing*)
I've been waiting for this.

MAN:
But it's true, isn't it?

GIRL:

> Well, sure it's true. And I know what you're thinking—there was plenty of time.

MAN:

> And wasn't there?

MAN:

> Well, sure there was. But you'll just have to count me out. I'm sorry. I was downstairs watching Papa fix the scones and I never heard anyone say a single word about what they did together in that room that first time. Nobody ever mentioned it. I mean—most people wouldn't talk about it, would they?

MAN:

> Young woman, it's not important what your mother and the injured man did in the room that day. . . .

GIRL:

> It's not? Well, heavens, and all this time I thought you were on the other side. I thought you were taking a sort of moral stand. You know—I thought you were suspicious.

MAN:

> Of course what they did was important. But I was merely about to make it clear, young woman, that the important thing—for the moment—is that your father, while fiddling with the oven and measuring proper quantities of sugar, may have allowed some similar speculation, concerning the amount of time your mother was devoting to this injured stranger,

to rise like yeast inside his brain. If so, the damage was done from the start. And don't you think it quite possible that some such idea, about your mother and this other man, might have crossed your father's mind in the kitchen?
(*He faces the girl.*)
It's quite possible, isn't it?

GIRL:

You mean that a little picture of Mama lying upstairs stark naked with a man whose name we didn't even know at the time, and offering him the golden flank everyone thought belonged to Papa, might just have popped into Papa's mind while he was watching the temperature climbing in the oven? Is that what you mean? Well, I doubt it.

MAN:

But why don't you admit it's possible?

GIRL:

You know—wouldn't he have burned the scones? If the yeast had risen in Papa's mind as you say it did, I think he would have burned the scones. And he didn't. And I already told you—Papa was just pure.

MAN:

And you?

GIRL:

I'm not a virgin, if that's what you mean. But I'm not proud of it. You know. . . .

MAN:

    (*pausing*)
I meant that you are rather like your father. You and your father had rather similar ways of thinking. Don't you agree?

GIRL:

    Papa used to tell me to be patient. He always said it was better to wait than to end up sorry. He always said the times had changed but that a girl still had the right to say no if she wanted to. He used to catch me by the arm and say. . . .

MAN:

    Hold on there, Hired Hand, what's your rush? You just wait until that fine little blackamoor grows up to manhood and you won't go wrong. Save yourself for that blackamoor, Hired Hand, and you won't regret it. The old master knows what he's talking about. . . .

GIRL:

    Papa had this virginity business on the mind, I guess. He said it was his fervent hope I wouldn't lose my virginity in the hunting saddle or on top of a prickly old bale of hay in someone's barn. That's the way Papa was—outspoken. You know. . . . Of course Adrian said that Papa's legs were like the legs of the Christ, so no wonder he couldn't ride. And that Papa was only bitter about losing his stirrups and wasn't really worried at all about me losing my virginity. Adrian was outspoken too. You know. . . .

**MAN:**

(*turning downstage*)
And you don't think your father had grounds for hating this man....

**GIRL:**

Well, heavens, they were just complementary.

**MAN:**

(*pausing*)
Three years ago, in the summer of your fourteenth year, there was an accident. The following summer you made full use of an opportunity to spy on your mother and father during the moments of what you call their tryst. And the following summer—one year ago, but two years after your mother's English friend first appeared on the scene—your father finally had his belated though revealing dream. And a mere few months past—in March, to be precise—there was the kill. I have told you the possible consequences—death, grief, anguish, a life of emotional oblivion—and yet you remain quite unaware of the agony of these three years, and even now remain incapable of feeling shame. Now, tell me—why did your father fail to help tend the injured man?

**GIRL:**

Maybe he was smart enough to see that Mama wanted to tend him herself.

**MAN:**

Why did your father fling his jacket onto the rhododendron tree?

GIRL:
> Well, heavens. . . .

MAN:
> Don't you think that the brief tableau you spied on might have been one of the opportunities your father tried to seize in order to win back your mother? Isn't it possible that he removed his jacket out of some totally naive and mistaken, to use your word, pathetic notion of how to achieve intimacy and suggest vigor?

GIRL:
> That's not a very nice idea. . . .

MAN:
> Of course it's not. . . .

GIRL:
> But Papa was always wandering around with his jacket hooked over his shoulder. You know—the jacket business doesn't mean a thing.

MAN:
> And has it never occurred to you that your father may have associated the blackamoor, as he called it, with Adrian? When he denigrated the little black iron figure, was he not also denigrating the small black-haired man from Liverpool?

GIRL:
> But Papa loved that poor little blackamoor. . . .

MAN:
> And hated Adrian, who was his rival.

GIRL:

(*pausing*)
OK, his rival. But successful or unsuccessful? You know—it makes a difference. I mean, I guess it makes a difference—at least to you.

MAN:

The point is that your father may simply have wanted Adrian to be his rival, that's all.

GIRL:

Then he wasn't trying to win back Mama?

MAN:

(*smiling*)
Win back your mother and lose your mother—both. It's been done before.

GIRL:

Well, heavens. I mean, I just don't know what you're driving at, unless you're trying to say they were all doing something pretty awful and that Papa was the nigger in the woodpile. You know—the real cause of the trouble, the worst offender. . . .

MAN:

For whom you could do no more than cast your pebbles into the void, as you put it. . . .

GIRL:

What else could I have done? I mean. . . .

MAN:

Wait. . . . Answer this question, please. Did you ever see your father lay hands on Adrian—take hold of him by the collar, for instance—and shake him until the man's face disintegrated into fear and confusion?

GIRL:

That's just ridiculous.

MAN:

Did your father ever strike this—rival?

GIRL:

Of course he didn't.

MAN:

Or say anything implying a malicious intent?

GIRL:

Papa was just opposed to malice. You know....

MAN:

But for three years your father listened to Adrian's remarks and the tone of his voice. And more important, vastly more important—for three years your father was either blind to the attentions Adrian was paying to your mother....

GIRL:

Papa was never blind—to anything.

MAN:

Or else for those three years your father was fighting hopelessly for what his rival had already won, or else was standing needless guard at the gulf he knew his rival would never have the good luck to cross. If this is not malice, then what is it? And do you know anything at all about the nature of the kind of man who could behave this way? I assure you, this kind of man—the helpless man—is actually capable of driving other perfectly normal people to desperate strategies.

(*He wipes his face on his sleeve.*)

**GIRL:**

Well, you just don't give Mama and Adrian much credit, do you. You just don't respect them very much. I guess it's convenient for you just to forget that Mama and Adrian had minds of their own and that they didn't need Papa to drive them to desperation or anything else.

**MAN:**

Young woman. . . .

**GIRL:**

And it's obvious you have no respect for Papa and me. I guess you think Papa was just an old empty sack loaded with venom, and I guess you think I'm the kind of girl who loses her virginity in a flash of foolishness on a wire-bound bale of hay. I'm not proud of myself—you know, and I don't believe in this privileged prostitute business, or the sacred whore or the miraculous bride, but Papa and Adrian and Mama and I were a lot better than you seem to think. . . !

**MAN:**

(*facing the girl*)
Young woman, I will not tolerate these outbursts. Control yourself.

GIRL:

>Of course it's perfectly true that Papa absolutely refused to help Adrian mount his horse. That's the one thing he wouldn't do. Mama didn't need any help to mount her horse—naturally—but Adrian wasn't very tall and usually had to have someone give him a leg up into the saddle. Anyhow, Papa would just stand around watching until the last minute, and then he'd look in my direction and shake his head and shout. . . .

MAN:

>Count me out, Hired Hand. I'm not going to give him a leg up onto that jackrabbit he calls a horse. You and your mother can give him a leg up if you want to. But you'll just have to count me out. . . .

GIRL:

>That's right. It was just Papa's way of pretending to be the injured husband—you know. But it worried me. I didn't approve of Papa making these withdrawal jokes. I didn't think it was a good sign. . . .

MAN:

>Why not?

GIRL:

>I mean—a danger signal?

MAN:

>So you were quite aware of your father's tendency to invent—withdrawal jokes. And you understood that this tendency was—unhealthy.

GIRL:

OK. But that's not it. That's just not it. I'm not going to let you fling a lot of psychopathology in Papa's face along with everything else. I'm not going to let you hang him on that hook. Because Papa was perfectly all right.

MAN:

Despite your own admission to the contrary....

GIRL:

It's just that I wanted Papa to do something—with them. He had his own little ways of holding up his end of the relationship—you know. But I thought he ought to try to do what they were trying to do, at least once in a while. You know. And not just alone on Gunpowder or on the veranda or in the garden, but out in the open country with Mama and Adrian in one of the fields. I thought his "count me out" business might just be serious enough sometimes to stand in his way....

MAN:

So you were quite aware that your father's impulse was usually to fling away the prize and flee the field—is that it?

GIRL:

I told you. He hated fox hunting. At least he said he did.

MAN:

He had a strong aversion for the despoiling of nature—is that it?

GIRL:
> Well, sure. Who wouldn't? Anyhow, that's what I was doing when I cast my pebbles for Papa. I was just sitting there on the end of the bed and telling myself it would be better—much better—if Papa wouldn't be so obvious and would just pick up Adrian in his two arms and put him on the horse—you know—instead of joking about how he wasn't even going to give him a leg up, which wasn't much to ask anyway. But I was just throwing these pebbles—and trying to help myself to see it all rationally for Papa. I just wanted him to get out there a little more and do something. I just wanted him to be sure to preserve the spirit of his own *ménage-à-trois*—you know. And I guess it worked.

MAN:
> Your father was with them that day last March, if that's what you mean.

GIRL:
> Yes, he was with them.
> (*She stares into the man's eyes and smiles.*)
> But if Papa was so terribly helpless, if he really was just a poor old paper sack loaded with venom, if he really did spend all that time withdrawing—you know—then how did he happen to be such a—perfect fiend that day? I mean, how do you account for his cold-bloodedness?

(*The man approaches the girl, steps behind her chair, stares down at her.*)

Smoke? Please? They always give the witness some water in a paper cup. How about me?

(*The man puts a hand in his pocket, with the other hand rubs his chin.*)

Aren't you going to do something about the fan? It's absolutely dead in here. That's all.

(*The man takes a step, notices but does not accept his handkerchief, which the girl holds out to him.*)

Well, Papa was just full of cold-bloodedness during the kill. . . . Do you have to question every single thing I say?

MAN:
(*crossing to stage left, then facing the girl*)
Did he carry a whip?

(*The girl smiles, twists the handkerchief.*)

You heard me. Did he carry a hunting whip?

GIRL:
Well, sure he did. You know—one of those things with a bone handle and a long leather tail at the end. He said they had taken away his privileges as Master of Hounds but that he was sure going to give those damn dogs a crack or two that day with his grandfather's whip. He said he had come along just to see Adrian break his neck but that he might as well be useful in the bargain. As a matter of fact, he was really quite fiendish with the whip that day.

MAN:

> I see. Brutal but accurate. And of course he was wearing all the rest of it—pink coat, black silk hat, white britches, spurs....

GIRL:

> Well, naturally. Except for the spurs. Papa never believed in jabbing punctures in a horse's flanks with spurs. Besides, Gunpowder would have gone out of his mind if Papa had gotten within even ten feet of him with a pair of spurs....

MAN:

> Gunpowder? Your father was able to manage Gunpowder in the field that day?

GIRL:

> Papa just rode him beautifully—you know. The sun was dappling everything and the air was cold....

MAN:

> The air was a kind of nude *glacée*, wasn't it....

GIRL:

> and all the horses were running hard....

MAN:

> and just over the hill the hounds were singing like inmates from an institution, as your father said....

GIRL:

> and Mama and Papa and I were riding shoulder to shoulder, following Adrian, who was a length or two ahead....

## THE QUESTIONS

MAN:
> and your mother, with her wrists cocked like little tawny angels, said that no one would ever suspect that this man beside her was actually a full fifty years of age. . . .

GIRL:
> and Papa pointed at Adrian with his whip and said he couldn't stand a man who rode with his butt in the air and that he was sorry Mama had given so much of her time to a man who was obviously at the mercy of his own butt. . . .

MAN:
> and your father, wearing the formal black headgear for the raven's plume and the stiff pink coat for the corselet stained with blood, said that if Adrian didn't fall and break his neck over one of the next few jumps, then perhaps it might be a good idea to send him home and let him kill himself in the Grand National. . . .

GIRL:
> and then Papa looked at me and smiled and said I was as brown as a blueberry—just like Mama—and promised never to call me Hired Hand again. He said I was just too old now for such a childish name. . . .

(*Abruptly the man turns his back to the girl.*)

> He said he would call me by my own name, which was commensurate, he said, with my beauty and the mockingbirds surrounding us on every side. Then

Papa noticed my horse's mane and he said that next time he would be certain to have the men tie it up in little green and purple ribbons—just as they had tied up Gunpowder's mane—so I wouldn't have to have the damn thing blowing in my face all day. Then Papa smiled and glanced at Mama and glanced at me and said that his ladies would have to ride just a bit faster, unless we wanted Adrian to beat us to the kill. So Mama and I laid on, like Papa, and over the hill we heard the golden hunting horn and we raced for it, laughing and riding three abreast across the green....
(*She stares at her hands, twists the handkerchief.*)
Well, the fields were dazzling that day. You know....
(*Pause*)

MAN:

Are you finished?

GIRL:

I guess I get my paper cup of water now, don't I? Here....
(*holding out the handkerchief, which again the man does not accept*)
Why don't you take it? I'm just tearing it to pieces.

MAN:

Are you quite finished now?

GIRL:

You're still trying to make me cry, aren't you. You just want to destroy the *fabric* of everything—you

know—you just don't want to talk about anything except how Mama knew more about Adrian—physically, I mean—than she did about Papa, and that it was all Papa's fault.
(*Pause*)
Well, don't worry. I haven't forgotten the life of emotional oblivion, that's for sure. You know—the life of emotional oblivion business really sank in. I guess you're pretty glad it did.
(*Pause*)
But I'm not going to cry. So you can forget the crying business, anyway. I mean—can't you let me off the hook just once in your life?

(*The man crosses to stage right, faces downstage.*)

MAN:

In the first place it was cold, quite cold. It was overcast, there was a late frost in the ground. Your mother's hands were raw and so were your own. And horses, dogs, riders—all were sullen and red-eyed and stiff with the cold, and all those faces, of men and animals alike, were frozen into long featureless skin-masks of bristling agony. Gunpowder was not there. As for your father—he was simply at home in bed with a thick newspaper propped on his knees.
(*Pause*)
Well, am I correct?

GIRL:

I hope you enjoy tearing up the *fabric* of everything. I hope you like using tooth and claw to just rip the veil. . . .

MAN:
So there was no talking on the morning of that Sunday, the seventh of March, when your mother and the man she had known for almost three years and you—the eternal chaperone, the go-between, the confidante, the last mockery of an ingenue—set out together for the kill.

GIRL:
We didn't talk much. It was too cold.

MAN:
And four hours later—four brutal and frozen hours after you set forth like a small and bitter army from that barnyard full of hickory smoke and icicles and horse manure—when finally you began to approach that shallow trench in the muddy and stubbled field between the creek and the stand of tall young birch trees where a few men were already preparing for the sacrifice, certainly you did not hear the distant glowing notes of the golden hunting horn. . . . Am I correct?

GIRL:
There was no horn. The only thing I heard was the blood in my head.

MAN:
As a matter of fact, you were thrown from your horse two times during those four hours of impacted earth and wind and animal turbulence, which in

part accounted for the throbbing in your temples and the tears that were gathering in your eyes. And one of those two falls even resulted in an injury, did it not?

GIRL:

A broken arm. But I didn't know it was broken. It didn't make any difference. I didn't care.

MAN:

Very well. We have the picture. Congealed clouds, labored breathing, your mother and her companion reining in for a quick rest and hasty cigarettes, and of course your own small tribulations of the day, and then the shallow trench, the crouching men, the sacrifice. And then—and only then—your father appeared.

GIRL:

He came running out of the stand of birch trees. At first we couldn't tell who it was. . . .

MAN:

But what you do not know, young woman, is that at a certain point on this particular day, the seventh of March, perhaps two and a half hours after you and your mother and her companion and the rest of your hunt club trotted toward the cold field of sport under a gray sky, your father simply put aside his newspaper, threw off the covers, shaved and bathed and dressed himself leisurely in open shirt and tweed jacket and woolen slacks, drank several cups of scalding tea and then, without a moment's hesitation, drove off in the ranch wagon to pursue the hunt. Doubt, fear, the possibility of smashing the ranch wagon into a boulder or of driving in exactly the opposite direction from the right one and having to be found and rescued by Adrian on the blue tractor—these did not occur to your father on that seventh of March. . . .

GIRL:

Papa knew where he was, all right. And it was joy he was feeling behind the wheel. I mean, just euphoria. You know. . . .

MAN:

Your father could have had no idea of what various directions the hunt would take, or of which few square feet of ground out of all the countryside the animal would finally seize upon for its martyrdom, and yet over the back country, lurching from one impassable dirt road to the next, he drove the ranch wagon unerringly, leaning now and again from the open window and shouting—Where the hell have they gone to, Blackamoor? Keep after them, boy, don't let them get away—until he happened to strike that one rutted track that ended before a fresh windfall in the stand of birches. And at that precise moment—he could go no further and had already flung wide the car door—the terrible bedlam of bellowing dogs and cracking whips and pounding and stamping and squealing horses rose on the air just beyond the veil of trees, and your father knew that he had found his way and had come to the right place for drawing blood. So this man—your own father—burst out from between the slim white birches like a maniac. . . .

GIRL:

You know—we couldn't even tell who it was. . . .

MAN:

That's right. Just some damn maniac or something, until Adrian poked his head up from the moiling trench and shouted—Look out, it's your bloody husband—so that your mother, who had not dismounted and was sitting her winded animal not ten feet from the trench with the sweat like a kind of beauty cream on her face and neck, and her violent muscles already composed once more into the shocking posture of a smiling woman at rest astride a winded horse, had just time enough to lift her eyes —eyes of the most intense blue—and watch this man—your father—wave at his startled neighbors and hurl himself—tweed jacket, woolen trousers, loafers and all—into the very trench where Adrian, like a little butcher, was deftly cutting the reddish pelt from the flesh of the fox. Adrian shouted—Get off, you fool, you can't prevent me. . . . But your father shouted back—Here, give me that knife, boy, and let the old master show you how we skin a fox down in Charleston.

(*He turns slowly to face the girl.*)

And then your mother smiled at these two men in the trench, which appeared to be filled with dry ice and flecks of blood and handfuls of dead grass, and said. . . .

GIRL:

Another knife, one of you? The old master has arrived in the nick of time and is going to help Adrian prepare the brush. . . .

MAN:

Exactly.
(*He takes several steps toward the girl.*)
You were trying to wipe your nose on your broken arm, your father was sprawling in the trench with one hand clutching his rival's shoulder and the other plunging into the fox's large intestines, and your mother was smiling and calling for another knife.
(*He walks quickly behind the girl, with both hands clutches the back of her chair.*)
In her black hunting coat, black boots, black velvet cap, your mother might have been some dark huntsman from another age—except that she was a woman and that there was no more wind in her face.
(*He takes a deep breath, stares out over the girl's head.*)
She was the perfect picture of a woman suffering her husband's disgrace—a picture made more perfect, if possible, by an enormous green clot of slobber which her horse, in a final burst of brutishness, had somehow managed to deposit on your mother's right knee.
(*Slowly he looks down at the girl.*)

Someone handed your mother a small silver flask of brandy. She accepted it, holding the uncapped flask in one hand and the whip and long reins loosely in the other. But throughout this episode she did not once put the silver flask to her chapped and parted lips.
(*Pause*)
Do you recall the scene? Do you understand what was happening? Do you remember what Adrian finally shouted up to your mother from his place down there in that disgusting pit?
(*Pause*)
Well, do you?
(*He pauses, then snatches the handkerchief from the girl, turns his back to her.*)

GIRL:

My arm was only fractured, so there wasn't much real pain. You know. . . .

MAN:

(*stuffing the handkerchief into his pocket*)
I'm not talking about your broken arm.

GIRL:

Papa didn't know the bone was fractured. He never did. But I guess it wouldn't have made any difference anyway. Papa was so busy trying to handle the fox business with Adrian that he just wouldn't have been able to care about my fractured arm. You know. . . .
(*Pause*)

MAN:
> By this time everyone—everyone except your mother, of course—was standing around the trench laughing and drinking brandy. And your father was laughing with the rest of them, laughing and nudging Adrian and shouting that they were all Mau-Maus at heart. And this man—your own father—in his by now torn and filthy clothes, even caught hold of Adrian's wrist and shook it and pointed and shouted—Look there, boy, every time we toss them a few little hunks of hot fox meat, those damn hounds grin and roll their eyes and drag their butts just like they're trying to abuse themselves, damned if they don't. And Adrian said—That's the trouble with you Yanks. Up to the teeth with sex. At that moment, one of your father's neighbors leaned down and offered to take your father's tweed jacket and try to save what was left of it from the dogs and flying gouts of blood. But your father merely laughed and said it was too late for kindness and that anyhow the soiled coat would be good evidence of what had taken place that day in the field. So the clouds grew darker and colder while your father and his rival wallowed in the greasy pit, stripping the white fat from the slender bones and cracking joints and squeezing small elastic viscous bulbs and yanking on cold tufts of fur and stabbing, slitting, slicing, poking, until between them they opened up the animal's little dripping coat and posed grinning together as if the man who had offered to hold your father's jacket had also promised to take a photo-

graph which they could later frame in black and hang on one of the hunt club walls with the rest of the pictures of the kill.
(*Pause*)
And that was all, except that suddenly Adrian made a final swipe with his knife and grinned and threw something—some bloody appendage—high in the air and shouted—Here you go, mother, catch. . . .
(*He turns to the girl.*)
Those were his exact words—Here you go, mother, catch. . . . And of course your mother laughed and caught quite effortlessly whatever it was he threw.
(*Pause*)
Are you surprised?
(*He walks behind the girl, grips the back of her chair.*)
Do you wonder that your mother was so—unruffled? Can you hear a reconstruction of these events, which occurred on last March the seventh, and still fail to wish that you had flown in your father's face and condemned him then and there before the assembled tribunal of wife, daughter, rival, neighbors, horses and dogs?
(*Pause*)
Surely it would have been better if you had.
(*He leans over the girl.*)
But it's not too late, is it. You may still give way to —shame.
(*He pauses, refrains from touching the girl, then crosses to stage right and turns downstage as lights begin to fade and spotlight comes up on the girl.*)

GIRL:

    It's not much fun to play in a world where everybody cheats. You know. It's just not much fun.

MAN:

    That's enough. You may leave the chair.

GIRL:

    At least Papa didn't fling away the prize that time. He kept it right in his hands until the end.

MAN:

    You may leave the chair. . . .

GIRL:

    OK—I'm going.
    (*She sits still and stares in the direction of the man.*)

MAN:

    (*pausing*)
    Young woman, you are—dismissed.

GIRL:

    Well, it's not my fault Papa didn't carry a whip or anything. But you know—he just didn't need to.

(*Lights out on the man, who remains a rigid bulky silhouette at stage right.*)

    Listen—don't you think he was sorry for what he did to that fox? I mean, Papa was cold-blooded sometimes, but he wasn't a criminal.
    (*She tries to lure the man from the darkness with her smile.*)

Anyhow, whoever heard of being pure without being cold-blooded too? You know.
(*Pause*)
Listen—my story was just as good as yours. I mean, they were the same, weren't they?
(*She stares up into the light, smiles, pulls her hair tight to the sides of her head.*)
But I wish I could have seen Mama in a wimple. Adrian just scoffed, but Papa agreed with me and said he thought it was a pretty good idea. Because that's what she was a—sort of nun *manquée*, which is just what Papa said when I told him about the wimple business. And Papa said any fool knew a nun *manquée* could never lose her virtue and that neither could I. Papa said we were all virgins under the skin, and I guess that includes him too.
(*Pause*)
But listen—according to Papa the silly virgins always beat the moral barbarians at their own game, so I guess we won. . . .
(*She smiles into the light, which fades to blackness.*)

## CURTAIN